CEDRIC P. HARRIOTT

Justice of the Arbiter:

OUR STORY ENDS WITH FREEDOM

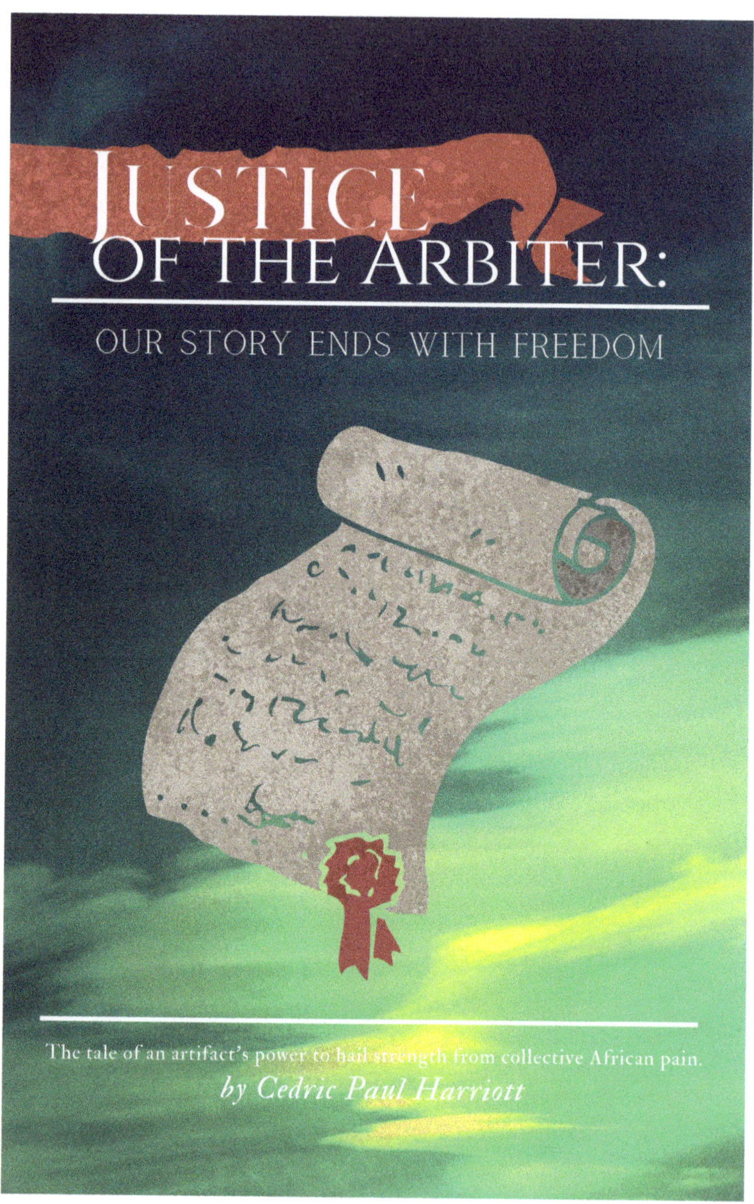
JUSTICE
OF THE ARBITER:
OUR STORY ENDS WITH FREEDOM
The tale of an artifact's power to hail strength from collective African pain.
by Cedric Paul Harriott

Justice of the Arbiter:

OUR STORY ENDS WITH FREEDOM

CEDRIC P. HARRIOTT

2019

First Printing: 2020

ISBN 978-1-951881-03-0

Cultured Melanin Literary & Visual Arts Studios
PO Box #4042
Baltimore, MD 21222

www.culturedmelanin.studio

THE DEDICATION

This work is dedicated, passionately, and wholly, to the collective pain and suffering that African peoples worldwide have had to endure for thousands of consecutive years; may you find solace here.

THE PROGRESSION

THE ACKNOWLEDGEMENTS

I first, in this reflective space, acknowledge the spirits of my ancestors. The ones whose rich history, from which I come, inspired me to bring forth my ancient melanin cinematic universe, beginning with this story.

I secondly, in this reflective space, acknowledge my great editor, who is also my mother. For she has helped me not only in my upbringing along with my proud and supportive father, but for she has taken the immense amount of time and effort it takes to help me beautify the telling of this story. Equally, she has shared a love of history, the sciences, our family roots, nature, and overall passion for sharing the lost African story with me. It has, in turn, enabled my vision to feel welcomed and provided for as if I was a painter with no shortage of quality paints, canvases, paint brushes, stands, and an inspirational room from which to create.

I thirdly, in this reflective space, acknowledge my father directly, and my two brothers who share with me their thoughts about life, the philosophy of everything, and whom pour into the quality of my life, love, support, generosity, brotherhood, and a love for our close bonds.

I fourthly, in this reflective space, directly acknowledge Keith Murphy, Anthony Browder, Asa Hilliard, and Dr. John Henrik Clarke for their most masterful contributions to our community – our village. And to the other master teachers who aren't directly acknowledged, I thank you and love you the same as I pour libations for all of you.

The Day is October the 3rd, 2034

I find myself in this lasting pensive state again. All of the answers to all of the things one could ever know are but plants in my infinite garden and yet I cannot share its fruits with a soul. I sacrificed the most human aspect of life during my journey to get my people here and I chose to give it up for the greater good of my people; communication. And sometimes, I find myself wishing that things were natively just. Justice being in a perfect balance with the justness of a just society; aligned to the most basic principle of decency among all living things. But as the philosopher Kai E.K. Maureantess stated, "The tainted water that feeds the plant, grew into our food and we ate all of that."

Actions, thoughts, decisions, the past, the present, the future, hope; life – sometimes I wish it were all something, …else – something real and… well maybe, in fact, I wish that the truth and justice were as easily brought forth as the evils of man against my people seem to be. Alas, at least now however, I am not too old, nor am I too frail, and I am ready – for you will see how our story ends with such freedom of being.

The Day is June the 1st, 2010 at 8:01 PM EDT

I'm truly excited to finally be done with college – is the expression I don upon my outwardly facing face. But in the silent roaring of my thoughts, the truth is that, well, I don't know what I am supposed to do. I keep hearing how normal it is to not have a waypoint after college but I equally remember constantly hearing that 'you're an adult now, figure it out.' Right, I'm a twenty-three-year-old adult who knows about as much about applied rocket science as an intern of NASA; it's all theories, papers – no application. And I feel the same way about life post-college. I thought college would give me more direction, more support; I don't know, maybe I wasn't doing enough myself but at least traveling the world with my friends should help me see the world from a different place. Especially since my past is so riddled with hardship and trauma, I think I just signed up for this trip with my friends to escape all that haunts me in the ever-roaring cacophony of screams within my mind.

I believe that mental health is so critically important. Yet, we as African children of a horrible Maafa, assimilated into a culture, air, environment, and foundation so foreign to our wellness state, that we find ourselves so incoherently disconnected from tangible healing. Alas, this world largely doesn't care about our trauma. I could write about philosophies until every margin, and every millimeter of space within this journal are filled with my tiny space-saver writings.

"Hey Andrel, get your head out of your own book and let's triple-quadruple check to make sure we are ready to bounce fam!",

Omar says from the next room. It's no secret I'm always in this journal so I'm always caught red-handed when people tell me to get my head back into the real world. Omar emerged from the next room, only to catch me red-handed with my head in this book, "You know we are doing this trip to largely stop living behind digital screens, writing pens, and other peoples' eyes; let's honor the contract we all agreed to fam."

I shifted and closed the journal then said, "Yeah, I know you're right I was just..." – but before I could finish my sentence my girlfriend Goddess also looks at me with her calming eyes and says, "You were just doing what you do, living in the many realms of thoughts you have, tenfold. Make sure you balance that out by doing us a solid and living in the moment on this journey, okay?" She comes closer, kisses me in the middle of my forehead and whispers to me, "Don't forget your medicine love, you know what happened a few months ago. Let's not have a repeat okay King?" Still in my own head, I reply a simple "Got it my Goddess." Truth be told, my mind was still in journal that I can't help myself but to keep writing in. It's like something has always compelled me to record as much history and philosophy as my muscle dexterity can muster. Besides, this journaling has been one of the greatest outlets for my thoughts that my therapist has ever recommended.

Anyway, our trip is tomorrow and I'm barely packed for it but whatever, I have my passport, I have my money, a bunch of clothes thrown in a bag, my wallet, iPod, toothbrush, my extra journal cause' I'll probably run out of space in this one soon; I'm good to go. I won't lie a part of me is nervous though. The last time I traveled I lost a massive part of myself through a horrible accident in Egypt but no one knows about it except for my family who are no longer alive. No

matter how many times I write that, or say that, or avoid it the same –
it still stings and the feeling of it lingers as noticeably as a bus-sized
hornet stinging me. The many lives I live, but we all have our
problems, our baggage, our experiences, right?

So, it's time to get some sleep, it's already mad late and my
eyes are failing me. I do want to be able to live in the moment as my
Goddess suggested.

The Time is now 10:44 PM EDT

"Andrel, bro, get up man you're a bit late on the wake up!" Uuuugh, thanks Derek. What time is the airport shuttle coming? Shanice responds, "At 11:15, which is like now, so go ahead and catch a shower – I'll put your stuff by the door bro." To be honest a shower before such a long trip would be life to calm my fleeting nerves. As soon as I walked into the bathroom, a smell of the chamomile and lavender homemade soap Goddess uses was fragrant and it brightened me up like the bursting of a thousand-thousand-thousand suns. That was truly a wonderful wake-up and smell the roses moment. I've always enjoyed those scents on their own, but on her, they just seem to put everything at peace for me. It's not even just chamomile and lavender but she was passed down this unique recipe from her family back in Ghana. She won't tell me what's in it but as long as she keeps wearing it and passes it to our daughter, if we ever decide to have a child, then I'll be plenty content, proud, and honored.

The Time is now 11:07 PM EDT

Walking out of the room I was changing in, and feeling great I took a deep breath, smiled and said, "Thanks for helping me family. I know I'm hilarious sometimes but you all are always here for me and I really appreciate that." With everyone looking back at me in appreciation Ashley, with her arms calling for a group hug, said, "Of course, we love you, we love us, we are family and this is a tenant of black unity." We always do this really warming spiritual tribe hug. We made it up in college and it has been a staple of our mental health ever since. I'm lucky to have these great souls around me; pouring such life and support into my wellness.

Omar, who pretty much took lead on arranging the trip receives a call while we are hugging and it's the airport shuttle. At this point, I'm a bit more excited seeing all of my friends this happy. I grab my bags from the door and head down the stairs along with everyone else and we head on to our first adult trip to so many countries. According to this fancy itinerary Omar printed out, we are leaving from Baltimore-Washington International Airport in Maryland, and traveling to the United Kingdom, Spain, Paris, Italy, Germany, Rome, the Netherlands, Amsterdam, and we are going to close it out with the country I, along with Goddess recommended, Egypt. No one knows that I chose Egypt because of what happened to me as a child there. I want to revisit it, I want to confront it, and I want to be there supported by my friends. Only when we get to the place that one of the most turbulent memory of my life happened will I tell them why I chose Egypt as the last country to close out the trip when the rest of them were heavy set on Ghana, to see the economic powerhouse of Africa or Senegal, to see the infamous pink algae lake. Looking at this itinerary, a part of me didn't realize just how many places we plan to visit over the span of a month but I'm still plenty excited. Not to mention I plan on proposing to Goddess during the trip on the sweeping grassy hills of the Netherlands; only Omar knows that so he booked a wonderful private villa for the day.

"Yo Dre', can you grab Ashley's last bag from the car when you get out.", said Derek. I didn't realize we were even at the airport. A slight unease touches me and I wonder whether I took my medication this morning. I don't remember taking it. Eh, I'll take it when we land in the United Kingdom and get some late meal or so because I'm not taking it on an empty stomach again – that never ends well for me. I grabbed Ashley's bag, gathered my own, and headed on in the airport. It's quite surprising how smoothly everything moved, well until I could have sworn, I saw a "colored" and "white's only" sign where the bathroom sign was in the area where we were sitting. On first glance I know I saw it but it isn't there now. I swear, the mind is a crazy powerhouse of material we barely understand.

Looks like it's time to board the plane. All my friends are even more hype now and to be honest, so am I!

The Day is June the 2nd, 2010 at 2:07 AM EDT

I'm really tired. I've always found the map button on the screen of the chair in front of you to be interesting. I always press it and look out of the window. The plane speed, the altitude, the flight vector, and the view from outside of the window that is sometimes sheathed by thick clouds and a blistering sun; it's always so beautiful to me. But I barely got any sleep last night and my eyes are failing me again. Looks like it's time to catch a few hours of sleep while nothing is really happening aside from us being on this plane headed to the United Kingdom.

The Day is June the 2nd, 2010 at 9:18 PM BST

"Hey love, it's time to wake up; the plane is about to land.", says Goddess. Feeling well rested but like I could have slept for about twenty more hours I looked at her and said, "I must've been really tired huh." Smiling back, she says, "Love, you were out cold and you were talking in your sleep quite a bit. Something about a temple of 'Ke-hay-ray' or something, and you said, something like, I don't want to go over there, and you mentioned your parents." Looking at her and smiling back, I told her I was having crazy good dreams because the sleep-mode level was clutch. To be honest, I don't even know the name of the temple my childhood accident was at as my parents never told me but I do remember saying I don't want to go someplace back then. Is it that 'Ke-ray' temple? How could I know that though if I don't remember it now? Is that actually a temple in Egypt? Yet again, the human mind is a masterful conclave of hidden meeting rooms containing hidden meetings with hidden actors at various times. Eh, whatever – I don't have the time to ponder on that right now.

The plane has landed, it's time to help Goddess get her stuff, get my stuff, and get ready to stretch and eat something. As soon as I got up from the seat, I heard faint ringing in my ears, sounded like a chant of something – whatever it was, it was mildly annoying. I probably stretched too hard and my ears finally popped or something – I don't know but I'm glad it's over. What I do know, is I'm hungry, and I could go for some bacon, eggs, and pancakes for sure! I know I am supposed to be giving this Veganism thing a try but I could really go for some buttermilk pancakes, eggs, and bacon with a side of hash browns; okay, I need to stop thinking about food before I get really impatient with slow pace of passengers unloading – it's dragging onward like a marathon of really bad music in a loop.

Finally, off the plane and ready to get some food we stop at an airport restaurant joint called Chip & O'Lara's. Given the fact that we technically travelled for seven'ish hours but had to adjust time zones and it's 9PMish here in London, we decided it's best to find something chill in the airport. Derek and Shanice are doing their couples thing in line, Omar and Ashley are doing theirs, and Goddess and I are doing ours. It seems like we all met in hilarious ways, ended up bonding closer than the space between atoms, and honoring that kinship for years. Derek and Shanice met at a library where they were both looking for an obscure book and there was only one copy. Omar and Ashley met after Omar spilled coffee on Ashley and he insisted on taking her to a store to replace her clothes. My Goddess and I met, well… Our story, while a bit turbulent is quite beautiful and maybe I'll reflect on it later, but not now.

The mood is chill, the trip thus far is fantastic, the excitement is building up even more now that we are over here, and generally all is cool in my mind which means in life. Omar and Ashley are ordering their food right in front of us and I'll admit I was zoning out just a bit until I heard Omar say, "HMS Black Joke." I said it out loud in his direction and he said, "What in the world are you smoking on Dre'? HMS Black Joke?" He was laughing but I looked right back at him and said, "Didn't you just have a brain fart and order an HMS Black Joke? I don't see that on the menu," I said laughingly. He thought I was making a joke since we were at a seafood-themed restaurant and said, "That was a terrible Dad joke and you're already thinking like a father." Looking at Goddess, he continued, "Are you ready for the onslaught of Dad jokes cause boy oh boy, that was a super-dose." All of us were laughing now, especially when Omar said that he ordered a Black Cherry Coke. While Goddess ordered for both of us, given that I am trying to be a Vegan and she knows how to order safe products for us, I unlocked my phone and looked up HMS Black Joke. To my surprise it was actually a ship and with a pretty horrible but beautiful ending backstory to it; the story of it ended with freedom – crazy. Now why in the world I heard that name out of all of the other possible names is beyond me.

Perhaps it's just a coincidence but that ship, I found out, was likely built in Baltimore during the early 1800's. It eventually became the Brazilian slave ship Henriquetta, and it was captured by the Royal Navy in September of 1827. After capture, the British Navy renamed it Black Joke after an English song of the same name before being reassigned to the West Africa Squadron. The crazy thing about this ship is that it was initially a slave ship that was turned into a slave-ship hunter. Despite its smaller size and armament, it was able to chase the Spanish slave brig, El Almirante for 31 hours before eventually capturing her and freeing more than 400 slaves. I was deep into this story and clueless as to how the hell I knew of it before I knew of it. Before I got too lost in the rabbit hole of history as I tend to do when I am compelled to do so, Goddess gently pulled me towards our table and we all ate, shared stories of college, and generally had a really good time together.

Goddess recalled a moment from her past when she realized what she wanted to be in life. It was the second time I heard this story but the first time was when we were first dating and I was barely paying attention as her beauty, mind, and my nervousness made me completely unaware of any true cognitive thought so I wanted to make certain I was well-engrained in the story this time. Goddess, in her own words, recalled, "I didn't know how intelligent my family was when it came to medical and spiritual matters – ones beyond what people can typically find solvent comprehension of." Her eyes grew serious, and she wore a proud and pensive face as she continued, "I mean, that's not to say that they were stupid by any stretch of the meaning, but you all know that when you grow up in the Western-style of world understanding – how we generally and unintentionally sometimes view other societies as primitive in their awareness of higher-thought. I was uniquely exposed to both as my family always made certain I knew about my roots and yet I grew up living the western way through public schools, experiences, foods, and what not. But the moment I knew what I wanted to be, what I wanted to do, and who it was my responsibility to honor, was the moment that my great grandmother in the presence of my mother, my grandmother, and I, looked directly at my mother and told her that it is now time you pass the legacy to the newest generation of the feminine apperception. The mysteries we have created, that we hold, and that we continue forward need always be passed forward at this time and your little girl is ready." By this point, not only was I well-ingrained in the story but so was everyone else, since Goddess is usually more reserved in her expression, especially through speech. At this point, none of us were even eating any longer; we were just totally into the story. Goddess continued by saying, "When my mother looked at me and reached inside of her purse for this key, she told great grandma Ellesenyia that she never let it out of her view, I was stunned. It was actually three keys and they were each different with one being a skeleton type of key, the second being a silver key with beautiful engraving of African symbols, and the third being a literal key made from gold engrained with some sort of language combined with symbols. I had always known that the women in my family were in tune with something more than meets the eye, but I didn't know what it meant, where I fit in with it, nor what the depths of their practice truly was at that time. I was just turning nineteen. I remember getting home and my mom opening up this gold box that she said had been secretly handed down in her family since before the time of enslavement. Luckily for our family, we weren't ever completely disconnected from our African lineage. Not to bore you all, but long story short, what I was eventually shown was a battle-tested and time-tested path containing the knowledge of the healing and spiritual arts although sometimes I feel like I am barely ready and I can't even tell you how many friends I've lost since allowing myself to become that which I know I must be." With all of our jaws dropped, we wanted her to continue but as she looked up, snapped out of it, and saw that we were all staring at her in amazement, we could tell that she didn't really want to continue on. Omar broke the few minutes of silence by starting to bring up stories of how him and I became blood-brothers in the first place. It was a welcomed change of flow and it put Goddess more at ease as the spotlight was no longer on her. It however, left me a little melancholy as this is where my nihilism and misanthropic tendencies begin to overshadow my sanity; both of my parents died. It was Omar's family who took me in and raised me as if I was one of them in the first place. I remember vividly the night they died but I absolutely hate talking, thinking, or even writing about it – even if writing it here is what my therapist says is healthy to do since I'm writing to myself. A part of me wants to just forget that night and another part knows that it wouldn't be honoring their memory if I did. Maybe, later with this journaling book thing between my head and with pen and paper, I'll remind myself about what happened, in gruesome detail, but then again maybe not. Ugh, I just blew my own mood. I'm going to stop writing here now and just live in the moment with my friends.

The Day is June 2nd, 2010 at 10:53 PM BST

Man, that was some good food and it wasn't even because I was hungry – well, maybe it was both. Great friends, great conversation, a great trip thus far, and great times with my lady Goddess. "Aye' Dre' can you order a car for us to get back to the hotel in Croydon?", Omar asked. I'm already half on my phone and half writing in this journal anyway so it's nothing. Omar, Shanice, and Ashley all went to the restrooms while the rest of us sat there, full, and watching the luggage with all of us getting a little drowsy. Everyone comes back and the ride has arrived. We all get into the car and head back to the hotel to check-in, decompress, and catch a shower before we turn in for the night. At least, this is what we thought before we caught our second wind after chillin' at the hotel for a few hours. We decided to check out this local Rave in the city of London.

The Day is now June 2nd, 2010 at 11:43 PM BST

We order another car to take us to the party until at least one in the morning given the fact that we have a full-day and we only want to see what this party life is about. The party is far more fun than we could have imagined and while other people tried to dance with us, we kept it chill between our own couples' circles. Goddess and I don't drink so while everyone else were enjoying spirits and other drinks we chose to have sparkling waters with lime for the night. We end up partying there until they close down at the crazy hour of two AM. Since the hotel wasn't that far we decided to be the dedicated driver-walkers and lead the group back to the hotel. But with my luck of occasionally losing my balance, I stumbled on a loose brick from the uneven cobblestone walkway. I pretty much completely fell but managed to catch myself before I made kissy-face with the ground. Before I could rise from this kneeling position, I looked up and I saw this haunting image of a man in old-timey European garbs. With a whip and a scowl on his face he cracks the whip over my back and as I felt the pain and flinched, he disappeared. Instead of the old guy being in front of me as he just was when I opened my eyes after flinching it was Derek trying to help me get up. Good thing four out of six people were drunk and barely paying attention to my over-reaction. Goddess, I believe sensed something was wrong and said, "Love, are you okay? I'm a little worried about you now. Are you feeling okay?" I lied to her in the haste of that moment as to not cause a scene so I said, "I'm fine said yes." I led her to believe that I was making another dad joke trying to play off falling onto the ground. In the back of my mind I wondered, what the hell it was that I saw and how I felt about what I saw. It wasn't even just the man's scowl and whip that I felt. I felt a name, it was Jessun Avery Smith. But who in all of the worlds he was?

The Day is June the 3rd, 2010 at 3:06 AM BST

I should be sleeping but I can't shake what I felt walking back to the hotel from the party – Jessun Avery Smith. After looking up the name, I found out that he was a slave who was beaten at the very spot where I fell because he allegedly didn't properly yield to a white man on the sidewalk. How did I know his name before I knew who he was? How could I have felt the whip across my skin or see his scowl? It all felt so real but it clearly wasn't. I really want to tell someone but I really don't want to be that guy who ends the trip on some spooky pseudo "I see dead people" trip. It didn't help that we had an edible or two while at the party so it literally could just be me having a reaction – at least, that is what I'm convincing myself to believe so I can get some rest. But I'm lying here and I can't get it out of my head.

The Day is June the 3rd 2010 at 8:01 AM BST

I'm one of the first to wake up it appears and while it is a bit early, I'm going to go ahead and get a few things from the store across the street. Finally, some bacon, eggs, and pancakes!

The Day is June the 3rd. 2010 at 8:55 AM BST

By the time I get back, everyone is up and doing various things. Shanice and Derek are showering, Omar and Ashley are getting dressed and Goddess is making tea. As soon as we make eye contact, I remember that I'm trying the road to Veganism so Omar and Ashley gladly take the non-Vegan stuff I got from the store. Goddess smiles and said, "Love, it gets easier. We live in a great time to be Vegan." Knowing she is correct, I yield and enjoy a pretty tasty breakfast with her. She made some vegan sausage, a few slices of fruit, homemade orange juice, and some oatmeal; it was actually really tasty and filling. Beyond just being tasty I feel it in my spirit. Not consuming the dead flesh of sentient beings feels different; better. I feel clearer.

Looks like the semi-plans for today include visiting the Boxpark, the London Eye, the British Museum, the royal palace, and some general walking around. We only got to the first few things today but there were so many extra stops in between that were awesome. We visited Camden Town and some festival-looking area that was like a carnival. Speaking of which, I'm getting ready to again live in the moment! This is really a fun trip.

Last note before I forget, some strange dude is around. Looks like some religious person but he is way off in the distance. I see some gold looking chain, some sort of hat, and a cream wrap around his chest but I can't really make out any details; it's a little unsettling though. I know the others saw him but I think they are too busy swimming in the lovely ocean of happiness. I wanted to write this part so I can remember it in case they show up again. Oh yeah, and I can't tell if it's a man or a woman, young or old, or whether or not the person is even facing this direction. But everywhere we all go they are within the frame of our sight and in just about every picture we took.

The Day is June the 4th, 2010 at 9:00 AM BST

We ended up spending much of the day in the British Museum just amazed at how much of our history was pillaged from our ancestor's homeland and how many people visiting there in the museum didn't look like us. While disheartening, we made the best of it and only decided to leave when we got to the areas where the museum showed the bodies of our ancestors; we had no interest in desecrating their memory in that way. We ended up not caring about the royal palace at that point and found our way to more side shops as well as visiting some "off the beaten path" areas of the city. It was a cool time yet again. As couples we were all bonding and as friends in this group, I think we realized just how much of a life-long connection we have. Anyway, its already later in the day so I'm going to enjoy the evening in the real world outside of this journal thing. Besides, we leave for Spain in a few days so I want to soak in just a few more hours of London. I'll likely be offline from here until then.

The Day is June the 8th, 2010 at 11:52 AM BST

It's Spain day! We are taking a nonstop flight from London to Madrid with a flight time of about two hours and thirty minutes. I'm not tired and I have the window seat so I'll be doing my looking at everything while zoning out standard thing.

The Day is June the 8th, 2010 at 2:52 PM GMT

The flight was really chill, the luggage claim was pretty chill, the ride from the airport to the hotel was chill, and our room with top floor views were awesome. Spain is truly a beautiful place with a gentle flow to it – well, at least it is from my tourist vantage point. "Dre' come to the corner store with me so we can get some groceries bro." Omar said as he grabbed his wallet and phone from the table beside me. Since we are only here for two days, I didn't really see the point of doing 'grocery' shopping and figured we could just get some basic coffee, cereal, and what not while eating at the local spots while we are in Spain. I didn't fight him on it though so we left and were our way to the store. I didn't realize he meant literally walk but Madrid is pretty compact where we are so it isn't hard to get to any place either walking or on bicycles.

On our way to the store many things caught my eye. But there are really interesting alleyways with incredible ironworks and colors that just speak to the hobby artist in me. I didn't want to stop on the way back while we had groceries so I took a few shots of some of the alleyways with my phone for painting and such later on. As I approached this one particular alleyway that's about midway to the store my ears started to ring. Thinking nothing of it, I get ready to look down the alley when Omar, pointing at a mural in his direction says, "Can you get a few shots of this for me since you're at a great spot?" He was right so of course I took a few for him and for myself. When I turned around and looked down the alleyway, I saw something seemingly out of place. They were really dark-skinned melanin-rich people with strong African features wearing these incredible outfits. The ringing in my ears grows as they approach. Time felt like it was either slowing down or they were just really slow walkers. I waved at them as to get their attention so I could ask them more about themselves but even though they were looking right at me, they didn't wave back. They kept walking forward in my direction. My ears were ringing even more now but not enough to shake my vigilant eyes being zoned in on them. Just as they walk into a light source in the alley someone bumps me from behind and I drop my phone. Bending down to pick it up and looking back into the alley, the two men are gone. But the ringing in my ears has lessened while not being completely gone. I turned around to look at Omar and he was busy talking to some locals so asking him if he saw me doing anything strange would have been a moot point. We kept going onward to the store and I tried my best not to think anything else of it.

The rest of the day we all visit some pretty vanilla tourist spots, eat some pretty cool local foods, buy some trinkets, build and bond with each other; generally speaking, we had an awesome time that led to me forgetting to write down the day-to-day happenings. This was a great thing to be honest and I don't regret it at all.

The Day is June the 10th, 2010 at 8:01 PM GMT

Looks like we have all decided to add a bonus trip to the schedule which is cool by all of us. Shifting hotel times and what not seems to be easy because we aren't asking for refunds and in many of these places, we are taking buses or paying for flights almost on the spot anyway so it is what it is – off to France we go!

Well that was the quickest flight I think I've ever had in my life. A whopping 'almost an hour' to get from Barcelona to Paris but I ain't complaining.

When we got to the hotel, I took a nap and it was a strange one because of the dreams I was having. I don't have much time to go through it in detail because we are about to hit the town but, in the dream, there was this place called Château de Joux, La Cluse-et-Mijou and it was on some hillside. It is strange because I felt like I was sick and hungry yet the environment was beautiful. I don't want to look it up right now to see if that place is actually a place but I will later.

Goddess suddenly walks by with her phone in her hand and says, "Hey Love, so I looked up the something you said while you were sleep. Fort-de-Joux is a famous fort but not for good reasons. It is where the French starved Toussaint L'overture to death on April the 7th, 1803. I'm guessing you're playing back something you learned in college?" I didn't quite know what to say so I agreed with her but in truth I've never heard of that fort and only knew of the basics as it related to the life and murder of Toussaint L'overture. Not to mention, how did I feel sick like I had pneumonia and why was I hungry? It is as if I knew – no, I felt – what he was going through. Now that I think of it the environment was beautiful as if it were spring. Something is clearly wrong with me but I can't place what it is and I am trying to hold it together for myself, for my Goddess, and for my friends – I believe I am failing horribly to that end. It's frustrating but whatever, I'm leaving to forget about all of this; time for some fun in the city.

The Day is June 10th, 2010 at 10:35 PM GMT

The party scene is incredible here. The music is cool, the people are festive, the mood is wonderful; life is good right now. As part of the music continues there is a moment where the lights cut out for dramatic effect on the outdoor dance floor. The low rhythm of the song continues and the crowd gets more hype waiting for the beat to drop. Eventually the beat drop comes and that is when something I will never be able to digest happens to me. When the lights came back on, I was in front of a sign that read Nantes. A loud rumble in body was present and my ears were ringing with pulses of frequency changes. A voice began narrating what I was seeing in my head and it was telling me how they wanted to show me France's leading slave port at Nantes. Between 1738 and 1745 Nantes transported about 55,000 enslaved Africans to the New World with about 180 ships. I was told that from the early 1700's to the late 1700's nearly 800 vessels left port at Nantes during the great Maafa of Africans. I couldn't even digest that moment and horrific scenes of Africans being whipped all around me, and so many chains; families being broken apart. There was so much sadness and despair; so much evil at the hands of the French. I screamed as loud as I could in that moment to make it all go away; closing my eyes in the process. When I opened my eyes again and stopped yelling, I experienced a memory that I tried to lock away. It was the moment in my childhood when I was diagnosed with paranoid schizophrenia and a rare type of dissociative disorder. I remember the doctors vividly. Dr. Lefkowitz and Dr. Jefferson were their names but this time during the flashback I learned more about them. Perhaps, they were wrong and I'm not crazy.

Maybe there's something wrong with them? Maybe, the pain from my ancestors is calling out to me, to all of us. Maybe, we are just so drugged and assimilated into a captive society that we can no longer feel the connection.

The vision ended when Goddess kissed me on the forehead and told me she was tired and ready to go. She said something rather strange as well. She told me that, "Something feels wrong. There's so much happiness in this moment but something feels like it is troubling you and I feel it. I can't explain it but it's something. Let's just go." I think she saw the look in my eyes. A look of fear, confusion, anger; pain. I held her tightly in my arms as she laid her head on my chest. She heard my heart beat slowing down to normalcy and we just stood there still for about ten minutes just slowly moving our arms around each other as we hugged.

The Day is June the 11th, 2010 at 7:11 AM GMT

We are taking a day trip to Portugal to see the beautiful waters on the shores and cliffs of Lagos. People both here in Paris and in the states mentioned it and they didn't even know each other so we figured why not. We are already here and not too far away from it.

The rich brown cliffs with shimmers of minerals from the stones glitter in the soft mid-day sunlight and the turquoise waters between them with their gentle white and teal cresting waves were incredible. They were second only to the wind that graced our souls and in that moment all was well. I closed my eyes and took deep mindful breaths of the fresh air. I caught a whiff of something rancid and I opened my eyes to see what it could have been.

Off in the distance, approaching a port there is a ship of some sort but it looks ancient – like it doesn't quite belong in this place at this time. I took out my binoculars and looked deeper as my ears began to ring. There's a feeling that human beings get sometimes – that uneasy feeling when something feels like it is near you or behind you; that ominous presence. My friends' voices around me became muted and distorted, eventually yielding to become a constant rumble in all of my limbs.

From the binoculars I see a person of color being beaten, spit on, shot, and eventually thrown off the ship – and it shook me so deeply that I looked to my right as to avoid the sight. What I saw directly beside me and in front of my face was a slave being thrown over the cliffs; I hear noises behind me so fearing someone would push me off of the cliffs I looked behind me and experienced one of the most vivid and damningly dark; violently turbulent and horribly sickening scenes. There were hundreds of slaves – bloodied, tired, crying, some being killed, some being auctioned off, some being sold for breeding, some just being used for the amusement of their captors. Little children, fathers, mothers, brothers, friends; all being bought, beaten, and sold.

Then someone, out of nowhere, grabbed me and when I looked at them in their face, I was so overcome with emotions at what I was bearing witness to that I fainted or blacked-out or whatever medical diagnosis is best appropriate for the condition. While I was unconscious, I heard faint voices around me but I couldn't quite make out what was being said – it sounded like my parents but I can't be certain as dreams are often hard to remember during normal sleep cycles but my medical condition is a beast of a completely different class. "Andrel! Hey Andrel! Yo'! Can you hear me? Are you there.", yelled Omar. While crying and in inconsolable despair Goddess says, "Love, wake up, please wake up!" At this point my eyes were open and I could hear them but for a moment or two I couldn't breathe or react. The feeling was as if I were on ketamine and cocaine. I finally recovered my motor functions and cognitive senses enough to make-out the fact that I was laying on the ground with all of the symptoms of a hard seizure. It was then that I realized, I hadn't been taking my pills. I suddenly realized that I didn't even pack my damn pills so these psychotic episodes and other neurological issues are occurring because I am becoming ever more sober from my stabilizers. At this point, there really isn't anything I can do about it so I'm just going to manage this with whatever methods I can employ to do so. Besides, I'm kinda' tired of these damn pills and all the routines that go along with them to supposedly keep me functional. I haven't felt this active since as long as I can remember. The pills and routines slow my functions and numb away so many emotional spaces and feelings – it's hard to feel anything when under their spell. It's rather interesting that I am also remembering vivid details of events and places that I have no recollection of ever learning in the first place. I tell my friends, as they notice that I am still a bit disjointed, that it was a bad reaction to my medication and I just felt a little exhausted. Goddess has a feeling I am lying but decides to let it ride, probably until we get to a more private setting. At this point my friends stay at the cliffs after I insist that they do so while Goddess and I head back to the hotel. During the trip she plays with my hair which always calms me down and after we get to the room we don't even talk – we just find our way to some really decent sleep.

I slept the day away while she did whatever it was she was doing as I was under the sandman's spell; she wouldn't tell me but I have a feeling she was doing some research into my symptoms, her family, her own battles, and general self-care works but then again, I'm just speculating.

The Day is June the 12th, 2010 at 9:00 AM GMT

We are in Germany today and I think this is a day trip adventure before we head off to Rome, which I am not excited to see as I don't like organized religion, nor the pull it has on our spiritual state despite its lack of evidence or empathy for others. Debates on the subject always seem to find me and I can fake well-wishers with religious inclinations but that's a conversation for another day.

While Germany has some beautiful aspects of its history and some pretty dark days from its fairly recent past a flood of a certain class of memories wouldn't leave me with peace. All of the visionary experiences that I was going through were of Black Germans living under Nazi rule and the horrible treatment they incurred at the hands of horrible people. Some visions were of my people being denied rights and work, being sterilized so that families couldn't be started, being incarcerated; the ills of always being the captive in every society. The irony of this is that I can't recall one tour we took where any of this was mentioned. A part of me isn't a bit surprised as this seems to be the normal operation of the world as it relates to Africans and people's wrongful treatment of Africans, but I digress as the visions themselves were something fierce and left me horribly petrified for the duration of the German trip. One vision specifically from 1937 showed me that around 400 children were forcibly sterilized. Those families became broken, as a people being unresolved and unappreciated the tension and harm grows – festering into many of our actions today. I won't lie and pretend that I am happy with whatever these episodes mean. In fact, I am quite frustrated with this ambiguity of meaning and the lack of knowing how to console myself, council myself, and resolve these deeply penetrating emotional states. All of us children of the great world Maafa need therapy; therapy by our own, for our own, with our own, and through love of our own. I'm beginning to wonder whether I need to see someone now. There are just so many strange things happening to me. I'm unclear on what is real and what isn't real – being that all of this is occurring within my own frame of reference perhaps I need someone to help guide me through these strange lands.

The Day is June the 13th, 2010 at 7:02 AM GMT

We are in Rome today and are spending three days here I believe, whoopie… ::enter sarcasm:: – Omar says something about using Rome as a hub to jump to a few adventures we have planned in the area.

Omar just told us a crazy strange story and while he is joking about it – it seems that was actually a bit uneasy. He said, "Why did this old religious dude try some crazy Hostel crap just now!" Without us really saying anything he continued, "I'm just looking at stuff in the window of this shop and I admit I was a bit spacy or whatever and this dude comes out of nowhere to say, "I'm too old, I'm too frail, when you're ready; please…" Then he tries to hand me some weird-ass red and gold cloth bag." Since he was pacing as he said it, sounding like he just ran a marathon his girlfriend interrupted him and said, "Calm down hun, take a breath, and let us know the rest. We might need to all be careful here." I just wanted him to explain the visual nature of the person so I could see if it matched up with the strange person that I had been seeing everywhere, and who was a shadow in almost all of our pictures when we were facing their direction. Omar was still shaken and was becoming even more shaken up the more he told us about it. I believe he thought that he might get kidnapped but he continued, "I told that dude, 'I've seen 'Get Out' and 'Us' and you ain't getting me caught up dude.' After that, I ran away like the smart black folks in scary movies – I just booked it back here. I didn't know if there was a team of people or what but my instinct was to just get far away from that situation you know?" It sounded like an innocent peddler to us so while we calmed Omar down, we truly put the situation out of our heads and kept moving as if that event was just as rare as it raining gold and diamonds – well – until it happened to another one of us. What made it strange was that it was at a different time and a different place. Shanice and Ashley went to get morning coffee and homemade bread from this niche shop we caught a whiff of during our adventures here. From the windows we could smell the bread, the baked snacks, and even the coffee being roasted so it was a no-brainer that eventually we'd find our way there. Shanice ended up going to use the restroom and the person approached Ashley and attempted to hand her the same bag, with the same phrase, "I'm too old, I'm too frail, when you're ready; please." She described his cardinal-like apparel. From his demeanor she assumes he has dementia or some sort of neurological illness and tells the barista, "Hey, I don't know this man but he seems out of place and might have lost his caretaker. He told me he is too old and too frail so I think he might need help getting back to wherever he is from." The old man and the barista, then sat at the table beside Ashley and the old man, ignoring the caretaker, said to Ashley, "It's alright Ashley, you aren't the one I seek and it's alright." By this time Ashley was bewildered by the fact that now he seemed so competent and even more so that he knew her name. As she is walking out of the shop telling Shanice the story, she has a noticeable look of confusion and a slight hint of disgust at the random encounter. After coming back to the hotel, where we are staying, she and Omar are jokingly telling their stories while the rest of us just listen. I'm actually glad that they are the ones who look crazy right now instead of me having another episode and taking all of the attention away from having a great trip for a change.

After a few hours of them building over this story, all of us enjoy some breakfast together and head out to have some fun. We decided to be more cautious, travel in pairs at least, but continue to make the focus of this trip having fun, enjoying new experiences with each other, and finding unique adventures to remember!

There's a beautiful small city in the northwest region of Rome called, Torrita Tiberina. Neatly nestled within the wide expanses of rolling hills, surrounded by the green leaves of all plant types gently wafting in the winds – their sweet subtle floral fragrances being complimented by the smell of the Tiber River waters. The view of the river from this vantage point is amazing. It's quite peaceful, closed in, and yet open; organic and airy. It's relaxing, like sitting in the inner meadow of a meadow within a forest in a gentle rain while the smell and sounds of nature subtly sweep your senses to a state of sublimity and bliss. The cab arrives to take us back towards the inner portions of Rome but the cab driver, through conversation, recommends going to see Nazzano. It's another small city near Torrita Tiberina but it has wonderful scenery, mom and pop shops, friendly locals, and sweeping views. As we left the car and everyone else was talking, Goddess holds my hand – I feel myself beginning to zone out a bit; the views are even more incredible here than they were in Torrita Tiberina. Goddess' hand slips away from mine and she heads off with the other ladies to take a bunch of group photos while Omar and Derek check out the local antique store for trinkets to take home. I know they must've asked me to come along because I felt them staring at me while their lips were moving but by this point, I was semi-zoned out in my own head. They probably assumed I was just into the scene, which I was to be honest. I don't even remember someone handing me anything, wait, maybe I do actually. It was some older dude wearing red and white – point is so now I have this bag of whatever the hell this bag is because I just took it and told him 'thanks bro'. I guess I thought it was a tourist bag or something. More importantly, when I realized that I zoned out during this experience, I had experienced what was one of the most vivid visions to date. The visions were of European nations of the day pillaging tekhens from Africa to use in their own societies. It was a bunch of experiences back to back but I did pick up on two them. Something about the Piazza della Rotonda and the other was in St. Peters Square, which I know is the Vatican. The second one I know of the location so I'll highlight that as a playback of something I've seen or heard before but the Piazza della Rotonda? What in the hell is that? And yet again how do I know about such a place I've never heard of. I know myself and if I don't look it up, I'll never let it out of my head so here I go.

Apparently, this tekhen was built by Rameses II, one of the most prolific builders in all of ancient Kemet. Originally this tekhen was part of a pair located at the Temple of Ra with the other being moved by a few various people such as Pope Clement XI in 1373 and again in1711 by Filippo Barigioni. Why these societies were so enthralled by ancient African artifacts that represent the missing phallus of Asset's husband, is completely beyond me. Given what I learned about this I was quite curious as to whether or not someone or something was attempting to show me something so I looked up the second one at the Vatican. It was essentially moved a bunch of times by various men again including Catholic Popes. It looks like this is the only tekhen to have never been toppled since Roman times. The irony is that Roman culture toppled the society from which the whole artifact, and the story behind it came from.

You know a funny realization that I have is that I feel so much more active, alert, and attached to something, …more. I've always enjoyed the Dravidian style of yoga arts and I've always been more than surface level with respect to minerals and gems; but, not being on those balancing pills leaves my spirit more, …open; more, …available.

I walked back to the hotel by myself. Everyone else had long since left which was cool because it wasn't far anyway and they did ask if I wanted to leave with them. I just felt like I wanted to get some alone time in so it worked out. When I was just about to the hotel and a good distance away from the spot where I saw this old guy, I started to open the bag he gave me. Out of literal nowhere, or at least it felt like it, this guy in these religious style monk garments grabs me. To my surprise it's the same guy that handed me the bag. He looked at me in my eyes and cryptically said, "Only when you are ready – for what is seen by the light is felt by the seen and the seen becomes one with the eternally unseen, in-between, interweaved, and that which is hard to believe." Too tired to make an overreaction, but creeped out enough to show visible unease at him stalking me I wanted to get as much distance away from him as I could. Without even taking a second to form a cogent response, I straight told him, 'whatever man, I gotta' go' and walked off while watching him in my periphery. I won't lie though; I am pretty intrigued by this part of the trip and I don't know why – there's something compelling me.

Being back at the hotel I feel a little winded. I didn't realize that I was out there well into the late evening hours. I'm going to get some sleep… well… maybe I'll get a meditation session in before I go to bed.

I noticed that meditation felt a bit different this time than usual. I don't know if it's because of the lucid feeling form not being on my medications, whether it's just random or not, or it might be a bad edible reaction – I did try some funky remix brownie and I should have known better. Goddess and I usually stay away from those as we don't generally prefer to alter our state of mind without the ability to first perfect it lucidly; nothing against the plant life though – it's just a preference and our challenge. I'm going to sleep on it, sober up, and try this again tomorrow morning.

The Day is June the 14th, 2010 at 6:03 AM GMT

I didn't really sleep well but I don't feel tired. I kept waking up and looking at the bag on the table. Time didn't even feel the same – it is almost as if no time went by at all. I learned this meditation routine from The School of the Ancient Alkebu-lanic Mystic Rites called "The Risen Constellation", which is a type of hybrid between their Inter-Personal Meditation and their Outro-Spective (or Speculative) Meditation. This time the mediation feels roughly the same and yet more intense. I opened my eyes and the bag on the table was glowing faintly. My ears were humming like a whale calling sound in the ocean and it was pulsing louder the more I stared at the glowing bag. In my mind, I was trying to rationalize this as the cars outside, the sun reflecting, me still coming down from the edible, or something to make quick sense of it all but it was all failing me because, in my heart, I knew, I mean… I felt it. I stood up and walked towards the bag and this is when it truly got strange. The closer I got to the bag at this point the harder it was to walk towards it; with every step, the force making me resist the bag was growing. It felt like at first walking slowly from the sands of a beach into the water and eventually trying with all of your might to run underneath the waves towards something; the resistance pressure becoming dramatically increased with every step forward. My breathing got heavy, my muscles were tired, I felt powerless and yet it felt familiar. It felt like I was back in that same moment when I was young and had my 'accident' in that African temple long ago. Something compels me and yet something feels like it is testing me – urging me to not give up, urging me to feel the waves and to master them as if I were a giant and the resistance a puddle. I got to a point where I couldn't breathe at all but I didn't stop, my progress forward was so slow but I was so close and I wouldn't fail; my curiosity and strength felt out of control. If curiosity were to kill this cat then it would have an epic battle with me over stopping me. As I began to feel myself passing out, I touched the bag and the resistance stopped. Suddenly, I could breathe and as I sat just catching my breath, I clenched the bag tightly. Then, I opened it. There's purple, green, and pink fine powdery sand with golden flashes of light in it; flashes that don't cease even when the bag is not in motion. As soon as I ruffled around it a bit, I found a piece of paper written on this old papyrus looking material – Honestly, I think it is papyrus – and it's old – like really, really old.

Without thinking I opened it and I saw the strangest characters I've ever seen in my life. There are six stanzas of symbols and text that each have six lines. I started looking for context clues, patterns, recognizable symbols, or anything that might give me a clue but after about twenty minutes of this I gave up. Frustrated by this roadblock and the fact that my ears are still ringing, I stood up, rolled my eyes, and noticed that I knocked the bag over on the floor. Some of the sand leaked out and as I went to pick it up, I noticed that it had a light lavender, chamomile, and lotus flower scent. It was familiar, it's the same blend that Goddess uses that she got from her parents who got it from their parents and so on. I went to pick up the scroll from the floor, with my hands still covered in sand, some of it in my nose because I guess I smelled to hard and something happens. I feel paralyzed, some people are behind me, they are women, their hands are soft as are their voices. I can't tell how many of them there are but I felt six points of pressure touching the back of my head and with each pressure point happening in succession more of the scroll becomes legible to me. I look up for a second into the mirror in front of me and the sight is magnificent. I can't move my head but I can move my eyes and what I was able to catch was six women wearing amazing royal outfits of antiquity.

I look down at the scroll and all of a sudden, I know how to speak the languages and symbols I am seeing. It is a combination of chants and ritualistic movements. I am compelled by my curiosity and by this experience, half believing it is a crazy lucid dream I read it while also performing the ritual moves. I feel something in my head becoming different. I take a moment between each line of each stanza and breathe six times because it just felt right. As I read each part and performed the movements various things within me being changed. The shorthand saying, "Majestic Ultra-Darkened Light of the Hidden Creator One" was repeated, although at this time I don't know what it means.

The scroll reads:

S1L1: What the light thereby sees illuminates all what is thereby seen.
S1L2: Dark Light
S1L3: (Sym) I call for the information transmutation to begin
S1L4: (Sym) I call on the unification to begin
S1L5 (AncientTx) Breathe
S1L6 (AncientTx) Upon the closing of this stanza spoken

S2L1: Finding the link-way is the forward.
S2L2: Becomes Balance
S2L3: (Sym) Celestial guardians hear me now in this ancient tongue
S2L4: (Sym) Grant me the powers of the MUDLAHSEE
S2L5: (AncientTx) Exhale
S2L6: (AncientTx) Upon the closing of my past self and life

S3L1: Finding the way forward is realizing backwards is relative to perception.
S3L2: As Balance Becomes
S3L3: (Sym) Balance this balance; for it ends with the beginning
S3L4: (Sym) Allow me to govern the actions against us
S3L5: (AncientTx) Submit
S3L6: (AncientTx) And upon the sight of the architects of this scroll

S4L1: There is and Just is; No Beginning and No End; No Forward and No Backwards.
S4L2: The Truth of the Circle
S4L3: (Sym) Let the ancestors shine the way; the truth
S4L4: (Sym) Allow me to serve, eternally, as supreme justice
S4L5: (AncientTx) Breathe
S4L6: (AncientTx) And upon the people, my people for whom I serve

S5L1: Your people are not separate from you and you from them. Realize we reside in your minds' eye.

S5L2: Perceptions Change When Knowledge is Obtained
S5L3: (Sym) And let ill perceptions fall asunder by the will of the just
S5L4: (Sym) For I see my path and accept the pain it comes with
S5L5: (AncientTx) Exhale
S5L6: (AncientTx) I will, without hesitation or mental reservation the same

S6L1: Let our strength, resolve, and power from pain – burn, like 1,000 1,000 fires tenfold and squared.
S6L2: Let the Justice of your Justness Become Balanced Relentlessness
S6L3: (Sym) And let the justness of justice rule over the regretless
S6L4: (Sym) I accept the gift, the curse, the darkness and the light
S6L5: (AncientTx) Submit
S6L6: (AncientTx) Serve as MUDLAHSEE

I feel, …more.

Looking into the glass my eyes change from their usual brown hue to violet and they glow; they pulse into neon purple.

The ringing in my ears has given way to whispering voices that are in differing languages, at different times, and with different levels of intensity.

My body can, …feel.

The rumbling of the floor that I kneel on feels like an earthquake and yet I am still.

This faint sphere surrounds me now and it pulses at different intervals than my eyes do. The streaks are white and the sphere is beginning to turn a shade of impenetrable pitch black with spells of translucent white pulses occurring more frequently.

OUR STORY ENDS WITH FREEDOM

I feel time becoming non-linear – the clock in the mirror isn't moving and the fly that is on the window is as still as stillness gets.

Time feels, …open.

I black out.

The Day is June 15th, 2010 at 12:51 PM GMT

I woke up laying on the floor by the window; the moonlight peering through the open blinds and the sweet smell of leafy fragrance from outside gracing me. Was everything just a dream I wonder. The scroll is in front of me and the bag is neatly behind it with not a trace of the spilled sand I never finished cleaning up. But it really hurts me when I move too far from this scroll. Like, what the hell is this about. Is this all in my head? I wonder. When I stray too far from this scroll it truly hurts, incredibly, both mentally and physically – it feels as if everything biological inside of me is having something pulled from it and within my mind, the feeling is akin to the feeling of thousands of needles drilling out from the center of my brain.

Goddess' broken purse is on the table. I was supposed to take a look at it but seeing the broken strap gives me an idea. The cloth bag and the scroll fit perfectly within the purse and I use the broken strap to tie it around my chest like a satchel.

I'm a bit scared. Perhaps there is something physically wrong with me. But I knew what I am feeling is real because every time I test moving the scroll away from my person it feels like something is being pulled from me or that I have some strange attraction that compels me to maintain a lasting connection with it.

My mind. It feels so much more alert; darting through thoughts like a cocaine fueled Adderall trip. Alert, yet I find myself staring at the points of nothingness in this room; pondering over my next steps.

Faint voices begin to occur around me like a whispering cacophony of radio stations three-hundred and sixty degrees around me. There are light rumbles occurring and as they grow more intense a hard pulsing begins to occur. I grit my teeth and scream in my head as I press my hands as hard as I can against my ears and temple trying to drown it all out. With no volume control on my voice I screamed, 'What the hell do you want from me, what is this you are all saying!?' But the whispering cacophony of voices continue to grow in number so I storm out of the room; stumbling over nothing and rambling various languages as I slip in and out of episodes uncontrollably. On the way to get some water from the kitchen my friends and Goddess are all looking at me. They likely assumed I was on the phone yelling at someone but that all ceases when they notice the physical changes I now exhibit. I know they see saw it but I don't understand why they aren't admitting it. Instead, they are just staring at me while my eyes pulse neon violet and my veins pulse with white, blue, purple, green, and pink across all of my visible blood vessels. Without warning when I drink some water, a light flashback of my accident in Egypt happens and all of my physical changes come back to normal. With my friends and Goddess all staring at me in fear, confusion, and sadness I explain to them what I feel and what I believe is happening to me. I can tell that they sort of believe me but I can somehow sense that there is reservation causing them to have disbelief at what is clearly real at this point. Perhaps it is because I've had longer to deal with this and I am the one feeling it that I know it's real. I open the broken purse and then the bag that contains the scroll and attempt to read it in front of them to cause the events of last night to happen again but the paper is blank when I show them. I can still see the symbols and text but they are telling me that there is nothing written. They already had a brunch going so when the oven timer went off Omar broke the contentious mood with his shaking voice by saying, "Hey, um. Breakfast is ready guys." I think all of us wanted to move past this so we all sit at the table in silence and try to eat. The others are generally eating just fine. Goddess made some vegan stuff but, in this moment, I wanted some feel-good food and Omar made bacon, eggs, and pancakes. As soon as the food touched my mouth however, I throw up and I sit confused trying to eat and not being able to hold it down or even chew it without being compelled to get rid of it. With my own denial being assisted by the others' denial I chalk it up to a bad reaction of not being on my meds and I eventually blame everything on it. The others want to believe the delusion as well so we all agree that my medication not being present in my system and without a proper detox, I am likely feeling effects similar to withdrawal. Goddess recommends that everyone else go ahead out for some fun and that she will stay behind to help me out. She is a strange one because she is a vegan from the south where the culture of veganism is still in whatever stage comes before infancy. She has always made things from scratch though so she ended up making me some organic soup made of potatoes, heavy garlic, bay leaves, quinoa, carrots, heavy ginger, oregano, and whatever else has this soup feeling like life right now. She even made some homemade ginger ale. In Goddess' daily life, she is a well-versed nutritionist, so combining the right amounts of earth elements for various purposes is her natural talent and passion. Her meal definitely had me feeling so much better and I'm really elated she decided to stay and help me get better. We ended up having some great quality time; ah, my Goddess. We spoke about the events that brought us together, the things we've been through, my overall health; so many great conversations. I almost forgot that she struggled, or should I say still struggles, with chronic depression. It's ironic that I always almost forget this given the fact that this was how we met in the first place.

We both met at the "Palms of the Healing Path" recovery center. She is diagnosed with crippling and lengthy swings of chronic depression that pretty much just leaves her without the will to get out of bed for days at a time. I was diagnosed as a heavy paranoid schizophrenic and after a pretty bad episode for us both in our own lanes we were sent to the same recovery center after we were stabilized. We were friends then but we didn't stay in contact after we left, a mistake we both acknowledge now that we are together. As fate would have it however, we ended up at the same school and took the same elective classes at the same times! From there we ended up finding an incredible amount of centeredness around each other, we found out that our political and social ideologies are the same; so many things. We are just kindred spirits and I feel so much better just reflecting on those moments here.

Eventually, night comes. It felt like it just happened out of nowhere but I know Goddess and I have just been chilling all day so I'm not even mad. I'm headed to bed.

The Time is now 10:08 PM GMT

So, going to sleep… I should have realized that I'd be doing more than trying to get some rest. The visions and feelings of the ancestors' pain flooded me and I was not prepared to ride this wave after having such a calming day with my Goddess. These visions were so vivid and I was so lucid. I felt like people were trying to show me their story and that I was living their past without being able to act or alter it.

The first experience was that of Mary Turner. I didn't know how heartbreaking her story was but it was gruesome and I felt every part of it. It was the month of May, in the year 1918, in the state of Georgia. I saw the date in a newspaper on the table in my home but I had already felt like I was in the south given the thick humidity and the scorching summer sun hitting my face through the open window in the room. My story is a dark one filled with inexplicable pain, inconsolable grief, and utter injustice. You see, there was a white plantation owner by the name of Hampton Smith, a horrible, cruel, unfair, and violent slave-master. After practicing such cruelty with one slave in particular he was shot and killed by one of his Black workers whose name was Sydney Johnson. Hampton Smith wasn't a good man even with the most rosy color of glasses and he wasn't a fair man as he was noted for unfairly withholding earned wages; he was the epitome of what the pinnacle of a filthy soul looks like and being owned by him was akin to holding your hand over an open flame and him telling you it will eventually feel good. There was eventually a manhunt to find the man responsible for killing the Smith and it resulted in the death of at least thirteen people who had nothing to do with it in the first place; a by-product of a racist policy being legal and just at the time. Mary Turner was thirty-three and she was eight months pregnant. By this point in the experience I knew what she was showing me wasn't going to end well but I wanted to be wrong – I yearned for a shred of decency but a part of me knew that it wasn't to be so. Her husband was killed during a lynching tirade on May the 19th, 1918. Out of rage, sadness, grief, and despair while also being completely fed up with the injustice, she publicly objected to it. Her objection ended up putting her on the police radar for not being a good nigger and just taking what you're given. It eventually ended up with her being forcibly taken to Folsom's Bridge on the Brooks and Lowndes Counties' border by a mob of 'justice-seekers', where she was hung by her ankles, burned by fire that ignited from the gasoline they poured on her and the white men watched her die in pain and agony. One of the people in the mob cut her stomach open and when her newborn dropped to the ground, they stomped on it. As if this weren't enough, they shot her multiple times. I didn't want to believe this was real but it was and I felt every single second of it – with tears in my eyes as her body was buried with only an alcohol bottle and cigar marking her gravesite I felt the gun wounds, I felt the cut to my stomach, I felt the burning all over my skin, I felt the agony, the fear, the pain, and I felt the jubilant eyes of the white mob as they actively partook in my decimation. There were young, old, men, women; it was as if it were a festival and I was the piñata with my child being the candy for them to feast on. Without being able to grieve any further for Mary, I was moved into another experience. I was guided into another experience and a part of me knew it wasn't going to be pleasant.

It was the story of Nat Turner. I knew this story and it hurt just as much – I had a feeling it would. I wondered if they were related by the slave names they both share from the Turner slave-master owner.

Perhaps this was meant to show me that overtime we have just become naturalized and accustomed to being the outlet for white aggression to resolve itself until it fulfills its bloodlust. That perhaps, over a period of time we would eventually begin to enjoy the fact that not only was our hand placed on the open flame but that our whole bodies were and that we would begin to enjoy it. It was a twisted and dark recall akin to Plato's Allegory of the Cave, the wall of shadows being casted by our masters was our truth. I wonder, by me experiencing these horrible moments if this means I have broken through some level of awareness that was always present and yet so elusive. Does this mean I am the slave that escaped…? Does this mean that the sunlight I found when exiting the bondage cave is the light of the ancestors enlightening me to act and govern myself accordingly?

During the Nat Turner experience, I felt, …more. I smelled the grass and I heard the noose being fashioned. I heard the crowds cheering and I heard the people in charge sentencing me to death by hanging. All I wanted to do was free my people, both body and mind. I figured it out that the price of freedom is death; specifically, not being afraid of it. That was a saying of brother master teacher Malcolm X and I remembered that from a video I saw of him speaking online. Going against the institutional systems of white aggression meant that my life was going to be short, but I didn't know it would be this short – that I would be subverted by my own actions that mirrored the white peoples actions against their former British masters; the hypocrisy of their white philosophy and their inability to have self-reflection at their massive shortcomings is jarring. Nonetheless, I was tried on November the 5th of 1831 and subsequently hanged on the 11th in Jerusalem, Virginia where I was also flayed and beheaded to frighten other would-be leaders.

By this point I couldn't wake up out of this comatose state and I was guided back to the ancient North African civilization of Kemet before the Greeks, Romans, and Persians who, at various points in the chronology of time, invaded and crippled her. There were graphic scenes of ancient temples being destroyed to make way for the new conquerors' religion. People were killed, lives uprooted, and entire customs were systemically destroyed. The mature, well-maintained luscious palm trees and the gentle cresting of the waves onto the shores being eclipsed by megalithic monuments ornate with masterful depictions of stories signature to the African peoples of antiquity; a true sight I was blessed to be able to bear witness and this testimony to. The peace of it all was short-lived as the invading armies of other cultural groups tore it all asunder and pillaged it for their own ill-gotten gains; alas, I was bearing witness and this testimony to our great fall – one of the beginnings of our Maafa.

As I laid there with my eyes open but unable to move more experiences and pain begin to overwhelm me. As they continue and my grief rises, something within my spiritual core feels powerful. It feels more intense as experiences continue, it's like a trickling flow of magma becoming an unstoppable river of scorching passion. My skins normal brown hue gives way to the deepest shade of black perceivable to the human eye; its biting contrast provides a caustic juxtaposition showcasing the extremity of my new reality. My veins pulse a sharp but faint crimson; radiating from my heart to all of my limbs, they feel like feathers of heat brushing against my soul as if it were kindling my soul fires.

There's an internal culmination within me that is merging or battling with various parts of me; an evolution of my physical and mental state is I suppose what I am referencing but it is hard to just limit the changes to just those two levels of awareness. A part of me is incredibly drained – tired from the constant bombardment of new experiences, stresses, moments of incredible power, and yet moments of incredible sadness. I want to find rest but only find myself halfway to its oasis. The feeling of it is akin to trying to sleep while running; utterly confusing and uncomfortable. At this point my eyes are becoming too heavy to keep open so I will close out this chapter of my writings and just lay in the bed attempting to make sense of this mysterious path.

The Day is June the 15th, 2010 at 8:01 AM GMT

I don't remember falling asleep but here I am waking up. I feel sick to my stomach; even more so than yesterday and I don't think food will help me manage this one away. I realize however, that I feel incredibly powerful and yet incredibly saddened – but there isn't really a reason I should feel either. I don't want to scare Goddess or make her feel like she has to babysit me – there must be a way to suppress this until I can better find a resolved state to first understand what is happening and also how to convey it to those closest around me. It would appear that I am always facing short moments of peace followed by vast spans of torment and pain; reflection and recourse – equally of my own doing and as a happenstance of life. In this moment I'll fall back on a tool from the toolbox of my therapist and equally that of K.E. Maureantess, learn your demons' names and where they live – then rob them of their sanctity and their power over you. I've always really found comfort in that one.

Everyone else is still sleeping and I am, at this point, desperate to understand what it is I am going through. There is only one person that I think can help me and it's the person that started it with this incredible scroll. Off I go looking for this guy. I doubt I'll find him but I'm going to try my hardest to track him down.

Everywhere I look I see his face – his clothing and his walk are an image forged by fire into the purview of my mind space and it haunts me. I must've run into the direction of fifty people before I got close enough and realized that it wasn't him and it torments me. In the moments I feel that I have found him I feel happy until I get close enough to realize that from resolution, I find myself destitute. Each time my drive, my passion, my hope drained from me while my fear, my panic, and my restlessness grew within me. I could feel it in my spirit. It was as if I was storing this unease as glass bottles of acid in my soul – I was fine so long as nothing bumped me or took me off balance; knocking the bottles of acid into the very fiber of my being.

I am losing my grasp on control and I feel myself slipping into the sweet silence of despair for at least I know how that feels. I need the guidance of this elder and I feel like I don't have that direction. From my uncontrolled travels I know that this is a core of African growth and power but I don't feel like I have that mentor, that teacher, that guiding light to shine my path. I'm tired now. It's time I head back and see from what realm, experience, or feeling I emerge – I wish myself good winds.

The Day is June the 16th, 2010 at 9:00 PM GMT

It's been two whole days and I cannot find this old guy. I haven't been writing because I've been so flooded with experiences. There are just too many to record and remember. There were memories of the last moments of Michael Brown, Rekia Boyd, Eric Garner, Trayvon Martin, Aiyana Jones, Oscar Grant, Sean Bell, Philando Castile, Emmett Till, Renisha McBride, Jordan Davis, Alton Sterling, Malcolm X, Marcus Garvey, Martin Luther King Jr. – so much pain, so much passion, so much will to live, so much fear, so much hurt, so much anger, so much, …experience and they are all fueling something within me that I cannot control or understand.

I have felt myself being choked to death in an illegal chokehold and I have felt myself being shot in the heart. I have felt myself being shot to death in my own home and I have felt the noose around my neck and seen the cheering eyes of the all-white crowds. I have felt and heard; seen and lived all of these moments over and over without guidance on how to process such realities. I know these are real people's stories as some of them I knew and others I didn't but one thing that is new is that I can feel their lives slipping away in their last moments. And in their last moments I am them and I am with them. The sadness, the surprise, the soul-shrieking pain, the unsettling death as their life pours from their body – I know pain a thousand times over and each time I feel my ability to know peace and sanity taken from me and replaced with an urge to exact justice. But I don't know what justice is or where I fall within its deliverance.

I'm frustrated that I am so sad but, I'm going to try and get some rest for at least once in however many days it's been since I've tasted the sweet tea of a gentle night's rest.

The Day is June the 17th, 2010 at 9:00 PM GMT

I can't sleep peacefully; tonight, or otherwise. My veins, they are a luminescent burning crimson. My skin, it is the deepest pitch of black I have ever witnessed; as if one was peering into the deepest void of space. Terrible visions are upon me now. They remind me of rolling thunder as they cause panic, fear, unease, and yet a familiar sense of beauty for I know it is for a purpose. Still, these are ever-becoming the hardest flood of experiences; each increasing in its ferocity and atrocity. All of them are equally terrible and jarring to anyone's peace-centeredness but in the same breath ever new rolling thunder episode hurts more than the one prior. And yet, I get stronger with each and that much I know for certain. However, I do not know how to manage this new reality. I feel that others are connected to me but I do not understand this connection or how to manage it and I am truly angry. My anger burns within my soul like the fire and light of ten-thousand suns multiplied by ten-thousand suns squared tenfold. I cannot stop this anger and I see all of the windows around me beginning to rattle in their frames; they will break soon. I see the furniture beginning to levitate and violently jolt; they will break soon. I see myself beginning to levitate and with every tick of a second of time all of these happenings increase with intensity. The floors begin to make sounds as if they are being ripped apart; the boards will give way soon. The glasses in the cabinets tremble causing an uncomfortable high-pitched noise; they will break soon. Rolling sounds of thunderous pulses begin to affect things outside as I can hear car alarms, people screaming, and out of my peripheral vision, I can see the lights on the streets below flickering. My breathing becomes erratic and my thoughts begin to turn against me. The once relatively gentle crashing of the cresting waves gave way to tsunamis striking out at the shores over and over, the shores representing my sanity, my grip on reality; myself. Slipping further into madness as the sharp waves erode my shores; I am losing the will to resist – ceasing to struggle in the quicksand and instead giving way to its will. I levitate even more now; almost to the ceiling, violet lightning begins to pulse all around the sphere of energy and suddenly time buckles. Everything is still and there are people in front of me, looking at me, smiling at me. I will never forget what they said because their voices were all speaking at once, in one clear tone. They said, "When you are ready, until then be calm our child, when you are ready." They faded away as I attempted to reach out to them for help and then out of nowhere my parents place their hands on my shoulders. When I turn around, they smile and I fall to the floor in peace.

I miss them so much. I haven't seen them in so long and just then they looked happy.

I hate thinking about what happened to them but when they touched me, I relived what I blocked away from memory. My parents were murdered by the Ku Klux Klan during the civil rights era – I was twelve when they set our home on fire. My parents were activist and so they were always the target of threats but this night was different. My parents were in the family room and I was on sitting on the couch between them when a Molotov crashed through the window and broke on the table next to my mother. The burning accelerant spilled all over my mother who was instantly set ablaze. My father reacted quickly and grabbed the blanket he was using to put out the fire but right at that moment a volley of gunfire tore him apart and also struck my mother. Their bodies fell right in front of me and out of sheer fright I ran as fast as I could to the table in the corner, when in my father's dying breath he said, "Do what we taught you." I grabbed his gun from the kitchen and ran out the back door to my hiding place where I stayed for the entire night as the house burned in front of my eyes. This is the first time I've ever written about what happened to my parents and me. The aggression of ill minds from ill-minded people uprooted the strong nuclear family from which I came and cast the rest of my life into a constant struggle of mental illness and post-traumatic stress disorder.

My skin isn't going back to its normal hue and temperature this time – the pitch-black skin and the pulsing vein colors are always present. I went to yell for my friends but I notice that my voice has changed and dramatically so. It is deeper, course, and for some reason I have a thick accent from some part or parts of Africa. I decided to throw on some clothes and to take a walk to further clear my head, besides I'm burning up and outside has a nice breeze that I want on my face as that is where the majority of the heat seems to be pent up. I decided to just throw on a hoodie and some light pants with a cap – I should have realized it would be too hot and it was. I realized that I didn't want to be in this hoodie or this hat any longer so I took it all off while walking. As I was taking off the hoodie and it just cleared my face so that my eyes view was unobstructed, I saw the old man cardinal! Relieved that he is here I ran up to him and with my soul jittering with resolve, because here is the one person that can surely help me, I asked him, "What is happening to me old man, what have you done?" He smiled at me and in a faint voice replied, "I told you, I am too old, I am too frail, when you are ready, are you ready?" At this point I am over being scared, I am over being half-hearted and I need to know if I am crazy or if what I am experiencing is a part of something more. I need to know if my suffering is for a reason or if my nihilistic outlook is correct in its misanthropic reality. I still hesitated for a second as I stared blankly at the ground. The cardinal says, "I will go now, you are not ready." He begins to turn around and walk away – he just about gets out of my line of sight when I finally dug myself from my overthinking mind. I really don't know what I should be doing but I needed to make a decision and stand for something despite not having the full understanding of what is a proper reaction. Out of fear of not ever seeing him again I exclaim, "I think so, I don't know, why do I feel like this? I'm always in pain but I feel, …different and powerful because of it." As the cardinal walks back towards me he smiles as if he is proud that I finally gave him the answer he was seeking. He asks to see my hands and its glowing, pitch-black, and hot to the touch. As if he has caught a second wind for life when he sees my hands he excitedly says, "So it's real. So, it's true! You are changing, aren't you? You have read it; it has blessed you with the hard decisions you will have to make. Your spiritual fire from within is burning through your dense reality; the calcification of assimilation being torn away; burnt away by the rich fires of your ancestral heritage. Oh, I am so happy for you and yet sad by the path you have been chosen to bear. I am not sorry, and while you feel sorry, you will soon understand. Embrace all that is going to be. I must go now but I will leave you with these articles…" The cardinal beings to reach around various pockets within his robe and proceeds to hand me a cylindrical onyx box, ornate with amethyst and gold, a letter, a key, and a name. He then says, "These, for when you are ready. You see, I grew up thinking I was making the right decision with the faith and works that I was performing. I was wrong, but in fact, I was also blessed. I found things that I could not share, things that broke me, that helped me grow, but it has taken so long to understand – to travel – to decipher what is real from what is fallacy or stolen; corrupted or misunderstood the same. And to collect from this, the true path for the one who isn't too old or too frail. And I am now too old, and too frail – I woke up last week and decided that if I did nothing then I was no better than a wise fool drinking the sweet poison of my own eternal stagnation sickness. You will learn of my story because I will be with you and always a part of your power and your pain, but not your decision."

I was taken aback by how clear and beautiful the expression of his thoughts came across. It felt like he worshipped what I had become or what I was becoming. It felt like I vindicated a prophecy or some article of history that he wanted to believe was true – although – he stopped short of saying what it was and kept mumbling about the decision and how he was supposed to help me understand who I am now. Apparently, I am no longer Andrel Desiene Jouleni but rather – I am something to be revered. I am some being of great power coupled with great sadness. I am no longer 'someone' but instead it would appear that I am 'the sum into the one.' The cardinal looks up from his rambles as I tune back in from being zoned out where he says some chants under his breath, then became a translucent glowing figure, and walked into me. I immediately experienced flashbacks of his life and I learned his name, Haile Addisu Abera which roughly translated to the 'Leader of the New One Light.' It was also revealed to me that the cardinal was born on October the 3rd, 1936 in the country of Ethiopia. A year later to the same date Italy, under the leadership of Mussolini's fascist government, invaded Ethiopia. It was revealed to me that Haile has had an incredibly hard life of struggle and triumph; he is shot at one point in his life. It was during his service to a rebel militia group attempting to resist and subvert their colonial overlords, the Italians – the group's name was translated to 'The Fire Event.' His brother and sister are beaten to death in front of him by the Italian conquerors. Overtime he envelopes himself in secret readings of subversive material and it eventually led him to religion. He became involved in the Catholic church where he grew from the humble ranks of being what is essentially a royal cup bearer to a cardinal. During this matriculation he learns about two different worlds existing side by side. It is the world of the indoctrinated knowledge that has been polished by the ruling class and the true information on the richness of the history from whence his people originate. It is finally revealed to me that the cardinal does not answer to the name Haile Addisu Abera any longer and that he prefers to be called something different. This reflection point was the last experience he showed me and it was a subtle one whereby he felt ready and proud. It was at this point that he began to buck the trends of the conventions within the church. He showed me books he came across, areas of knowledge he wasn't supposed to see, and explored various regions of the world to collect knowledge. He showed me he couldn't get to the Vatican archives but that he made his decision on what path he was compelled to take. I came back into my own self and placed the artifacts the cardinal gave me in various pockets on my person. The cardinal, from within my own headspace said, "Good job, you are growing, do not call me cardinal." I realized at that moment that he never told me the name that he preferred to be called. The cardinal simply told me, "In due time, when you are ready but for now call me the 'The First Eye.'

The First Eye then told me that the key and the name lead to a home in a castle. He pushed me to find it by calling upon his memories to obtain the knowledge. Without truly trying too hard I was able to find it – I think he assisted because I don't feel that I did anything outside of trying to travel within my own self to see his particular set of memories.

I knocked on the door and spoke the name through the intercom box at the gate. This wasn't a regular mass-produced wrought iron gate either. It was truly handmade by a talented artisan of the craft. The First Eye told me it originated from the family of talented ironsmiths called the Simmons. It was made over the span of thirty years with iron taken from the special part of the world that each aspect of the gates represents. Specifically, the leader of this master iron-mason guild was Phillip Simmons who worked alongside his nephew Carlton Simmons. They created a gate that was ornate with lotus flowers on the far-left side, coupled with Kemetic pillars and Neteru. It transitioned in the middle to various landmasses of African heritage and in the center of it was a massive Sankofa bird. Above it was the heart-symbol of Sankofa and below it was the same tied into roots leading to the outline of the ironworks. On the right side of it were symbols and figures I knew nothing about. The First Eye told me only one part of the symbols wording, it said, "The Council of Kerrhe." I cannot believe it said the Council of Kerrhe! I immediately thought back to what Goddess said to me that I mentioned in my dream on the flight over to the United Kingdom.

"Was this the temple that I had my experienced from in my childhood?" I asked The First Eye and he told me, "Take my pains in silence; when you are ready all will be revealed." It's 11:52 PM and I will never forget this moment. A car drove down from the castle to the main gate and the main gate opened. A butler exited the car and knelt to me. With reverence and honor, he said, "Welcome home your Excellency, it is an absolute honor to see the one with Mudlahsee." I don't know what a Mudlahsee is though. I was strangely confident after my dealings with The First Eye and so I told him I do not yet understand what I am but I was told to come here by The First Eye and to speak these things to you and that you would understand. He rose from kneeling and said, "Of course, please." He opened the door for me and I got into the car. He drove it back to the house and as he opened the door to let me out, I reached out to shake his hand. He bowed his head, knelt, and opened his hands in offering. When I touched his hands to bring him back up as I don't need anyone kneeling for me, I learned his story from The First Eye. I was shown why I am revered as his Excellency and the Mudlahsee. The First Eye shows me that he is not a butler but rather a pillar of support, and they are called, 'The Ears of the First Eye.' The First Eye told me that this person's name was Dessen. Dessen then says, "My role in this is to show you all that is yours. To assist you in the tough decisions you will have to make soon our Mudlahsee. I am here to assist in making your transition to power and protection as easy as I can. It has taken us much time to find someone the scroll accepts."

Dessen shows me an overview of the home but not its history or the meaning of the front gates and the heavy seclusion of this castle. It didn't even appear on the navigation maps as an address. Dessen, shows me my room and tells me that him and three others are always on his call, that the castle is provisioned always, and that there is nothing he need do unless he so wishes to do so. I am interested to learn about this new role in my life and to realize that I am not, in fact, crazy. There is nothing ill with me that society needed to fix but rather it subjected me to forced assimilation to fit into a society that is out of alignment with the history and culture of my people. I wasn't sick, the environment was sick and I am now free from its grasp.

There are so many books and reference notes in my room left by The First Eye. The first one I read through was a few pages on the process of channeling people and their memories as I meditate. It mentions that this process only works for the Mudlahsee, of which I am now. After performing a test of it to channel the memories of my mother and father I notice that the deeper the meditation, the stronger the connection.

I also noticed something that I didn't completely realize before – that the pain and passion of all of the transgressions done to my people make me more powerful and yet they tear my resolve apart. Only one with the truest form can properly handle the pressure that the scroll extracts from the holder. The price that one must be willing to pay for ultimate power is ultimate pain; no great treasure should come without great struggle. Life just got more real than I could have ever imagined. You mean to tell me that the more harm is done to African peoples across the world and the span of all time – the more powerful and unstoppable I become? What happens if one achieves peace and there are no more transgressions? I channeled The First Eye to ask and he told me, "Your powers have a minimum level which is still quite strong. It is bound to the unified powers of the members of the Council of Kerrhe that sacrificed themselves to create the scroll." I wanted to know more about them so I asked what their powers were and who they were. The First Eye essentially told me they were a six-member council of African warrior God priests from various parts of the continent. While African kingdoms of antiquity were traditionally ruled by males, the women Kerrhe council members were part of a more secretive order of women that have a unique connection to the other spatial states. They sacrificed their powers into a ritual and a scroll for the defense of the African way of life – it was the formation of an arbiter of justice. They created this during the time period that Kemet was finally decimated allowing the gates that once defended the whole of Africa from foreign assault to come to pass. I am not certain what happened to the scroll after they created it but I can assume it was nothing good since The First Eye revealed to me that he obtained it from an oversight error with the Vatican archives transition team that no one is supposed to see as they are like whispers in deep space. I am glad it is back in the control of the society it was meant for. The First Eye told me that the deepest parts of the church were trying to figure out what the scroll was and just how to break the spiritual encryption that it was bound to because none of them could see any words on it and yet the resistance it had when one tried to touch it was of great mystery. I should be cautious about this. There is nothing more dangerous than too much trust, exposure, a lack of reasonable operational security; pretty much there will be danger on this path – people will envy what I hold and others will want to subdue me.

The Time is now 3:06 AM GMT

I went to my phone and saw that I had eighteen missed calls from my friends likely wondering just where I disappeared to. Its 3:06 AM now so I am not surprised given that tomorrow is a travel day, I took a little bit of a nap and woke up at 7:02 AM. I didn't call back anyone else but Goddess and I asked her to come to the address of the castle where I had been taken. She doesn't quite understand or see anything on the maps application but I told her to just trust me to never guide her in an improper form. Dessen was adding books into the study next to the window I was standing in front of so he heard much of my conversation.

He offered to pick them up using the "Ruby Fleet." Dessen saw that I had a look of bewilderment on my face so he asked me to follow him, which I did. Goddess was still on the phone and likely just as bewildered as I was – I feel that she was a little more at peace so long as I was sitting on the phone with her. I should have known that with this great castle inspired by African creativity, culture, and honor it would come equipped with its own transportation system. The Ruby Fleet is a motorcade of crimson Bentley vehicles; low-profile and yet still as majestic as the power exuded by Mansa Musa during his travels. Dessen opened the door to the middle vehicle, I got inside, and proceeded to pick up my friends and my Goddess from the hotel. I called them again and told them to have all of their bags packed and to trust me that I would take care of everything else when I make my arrival.

When we arrived at the hotel all of the eyes were on the vehicles. The drivers pulled up in a line at the front entrance of the hotel. Some of the security detail exited their vehicles and protected the interior vehicles from people getting too close, threats, or any other perimeter breach. Admittedly, it is going to take some getting used to but given the seriousness of this path I am now on, I will certainly need all of the protection I can get when I want to lower my guard. The hotel busboys, people leaving the hotel, bystanders on the street, and some of the staff came outside to see who it was but I didn't exit the vehicle yet and instead called my friends. The bystanders likely thought it was some dignitary or diplomat arriving; perhaps even a celebrity or something. Instead they'll see some regular young black millennials having a great time. To be honest, we will probably look like celebrities or royalty from Africa but I am actually fine with the latter more than the former. I told my friends to come downstairs and to leave their packed bags in the room. They all came down and when I saw them in the lobby, I called Goddess and told them to walk outside the front entrance. I had the driver open my door where I stepped out and flagged them down. They were completely stunned as was everyone else. It was even more special when I had my detail open the third Bentley door and told them we will talk later but to please head to their vehicles. They are all stunned, excited, confused, and yet trusting of my calm demeanor. It's likely they are more curious as to what in the world I'm doing with this but they will soon find out when I take them to my new home. I didn't even have to let Goddess know that she rides with me; we have an unspoken vibe that just makes it a natural known fact of life that when we ride, we ride together. By this point a crowd formed around us and people were taking pictures until we got into the cars and they could no longer see us. We drove off at a relatively casual pace in all of the vehicles and I just looked at Goddess smiling curiously. She looked back and said, "What in the world is going on my love?" I simply smiled more and told her that I'd tell in due time when she's ready. I laughed and told her I was joking; another Dad joke but it's an inside joke between The First Eye and I so I failed but whatever. She was just happy that I was happy and went with it. During the ride I told her everything but only got through about a quarter of the journey since we left the hotel. A part of her, I believe, always knew something was different with me during this trip. I only got to explaining about who the mysterious person we saw before was and how that linked to our friends' experience with the same person. I'll tell her the rest in front of everyone now that we are back – I can tell her eyes are scanning everything and now she is only half listening to me. The size of the castle, its location, the gates; it's all a bit much to take in. This is especially the case when the gates open and we begin driving the ornate cobblestone street lined with sixty-foot Italian Cypress trees, sweeping meadows with hills, and rich gardens as well as other castle annex buildings. I held her hand, looked at her, and when she looked at me, I told her this was now my home.

The Time is now 8:01 AM GMT

As the castle kitchen staff make us breakfast, I tell all of my friends to please have a seat while I explain what all of this is, why all of this is, and where they will hopefully fit within it. I explained to them the entire backstory of my experiences since we arrived at BWI airport. They realize I am not crazy and the look of gentle relief on their faces was as comforting to me as it was to their soul. Omar told me they were going to cancel the rest of the trip or at least get me to a medical facility here to really get a full-checkup. I would have appreciated the offer but I am glad they didn't do that. Someone I have accidently channeled and whose name is sheathed from me once said that success without struggle is ill-earned and ill-fated. My trials leading to this path have certainly been muddled with hardships but I see clearly now and nothing will ever affect that again.

They, now hearing such clarity in my thoughts and actions are incredibly captivated by my speech to them about who and what I am. My speaking tones, my thickened African accent, and the style syntax of my phrasings are all a product of the many lives I've lived through others memories; by collecting these points of strength and unique perspectives I am able to captivate and inspire our people. It is at this point I also remove the clothing, the gloves, the hat, the scarf; everything that was covering me and I take a few deep breaths. My veins activate, and I call upon my protective sphere to solidify that I am sane, powerful, and here for a higher calling now.

OUR STORY ENDS WITH FREEDOM

Breakfast arrives and they notice everyone kneels to me. I decided that I wanted to change that while still keeping the respect factor there to honor the history from which it hails. I simply modernize it for the staff living on or supporting the castle grounds. We simply instead, do a dap and keep it moving from there. We all sit down, and as the food is brought out my friends that aren't vegan ask what is it and if I have anything else. I told them that my… that our spiritual connection is not well-kindled if I allow the dead flesh of sentient beings within our portals of communication. On these castle grounds there will be no suffering of our animal friends here, and all foods are health-centric – this is a place of knowledge, rest, refreshment, healing, contemplation, and the overall principles of HOREMAKHET. I can see they are a bit confused but I told them to just give it a try and if they didn't like it, the staff would be happy to find something they did like, to which they agreed.

They aren't my house-staff in a way that lowers their dignity either. They are the support for the mission that we all serve. They all live here in a private community on the property, they are all paid six-figure salaries, their children are all taken care of here; life is all about peace, prosperity, health, and wellness here. These groups are collectively called, 'The Grounding Fires.' We Africans within this castle will do great things and in order to do so we must start from within our own homes, in our own communities, and within the relationships we have with each other.

We conclude breakfast and it is then that the conversations get a bit more tense. The power that I have is largely unknown to them but what I should do with it and where they fit within this painting causes a higher level of contention than I thought was appropriate. I believe that most of us Africans, whether in America or otherwise, play out in our minds what we would do if granted such abilities. However, now that it has become more than just a play in the recital hall of our imagination, the reality and severity of the decisions become ever more present. Ashley wants me to be a super hero – the highly public unifying symbol of heroism and a living monument of pride for our people worldwide. Omar wants me to be the militant-minded unifier – using more aggressive means to immediately quell any dissent among who the hammer of justice is for African peoples. Derek wants me to be the policy-based change for our people – using my powers instead as a last resort, preferring to be more of a hero representative of his people's collective interest. Shanice wants me to exact economic justice – electing to establish our own forms of trade and barter as well as instituting a living 'Global Afro-Constitution.' And Goddess sits silently but smiling at me with a look of pride on her face. As my friends all debate the best path forward and Goddess and I stare at each other, I tell them all that this is why I need them here but that we have to do this work in a way that is healthy for the mission we all support. These are great starting points for vetting a path forward but they are just the idea without even a foundation. They asked what the mission was and that's when I asked them, 'We need to truly define that first don't we? We need to decipher just what that is before we can determine where our roles are within it.'

I felt as though a part of me was channeling the essence of the great master teacher, Dr. John Henrik Clarke. I learned a great deal from him; spending a great deal of time listening to the audio versions of his speeches while working, driving, and even at the gym. He gave us many speeches and wrote plenty of great books – one of my favorites was the speech 'Christopher Columbus and the African Holocaust.' He spoke about many pensive points of reflection but the one I was pulling from in this moment was when he spoke on the fact that not all works should be done by direct leadership but equally by focusing on living it, growing it, and tapping into others how to govern matters of any civilization. Still pulling from the inspiration of Dr. Clarke I said, "We need clarity. Clarity driven by living the works and finding the best path of how to govern matters of a new civilization. I cannot do this alone and I barely understand the path that I am on so, instead of spirited debate, why don't we collect information relevant to how best to govern and establish a progressive society for our people." Derek interjects, "We get it now. What can we do to help? What do you want us to do bruh'?" I smiled and said, "Learn about philosophy, archaeology, history, mysticism, all of the sciences – find the youthful minds and task groups to be the new masters of knowledge with respect to certain fields. Tell group A, you all will be the wise people of literary sciences, tell group B, you all will be the wise people of military sciences, tell group C, you all will be the wise people of government. I think this is the clear path of foundational work that will help us find who we currently are so that we may discover who we must be." The argument subsides in peace. I tell them to take the day and explore the city. I then ask the security detail and one driver to take them wherever they all want to go. They asked if I was coming and I let them know that, 'I have something I want to do first but that I'd join them in a little while. I also told Goddess to enjoy the travel vacation especially now that they know I am okay. I could still sense some hesitancy in their voices but I told them we have limitless time to talk and for you all to hear my long-winded stories of reflection. Today, decompress and have some fun!' Since they still had some hesitation on their face I told them, 'Listen, I need to read, to meditate, to practice, to rest, to gather my thoughts alone; I have things to do that I need to do on my own first and I would appreciate it if I could have just a little bit of space to do the work.' Once they heard that, they were happy to give me that space and went out to enjoy whatever they wanted to do on the town.

The Time is now 12:06 PM GMT

I need to practice now. It is time to channel the ones who can assist me. It is time now to begin building connections in my head. It is now time to begin because I am not too old, I am not too frail, and I am ready.

The Time is now 7:02 PM GMT

My friends came back not too long ago and they have decided to cancel the rest of the trip. It doesn't bother me as we have the ability to go wherever we want at any moment so that isn't an issue that concerns me. They also decided to stay with me and to help me support this mission. What I didn't know is that they went out on the town but spent the entire day gathering information to help me navigate the trials I am certain to face. This brought me to tears. I knew they were great friends but this was just too much to take and it was so beautiful that I buckled down and cried harder than I ever have before. That caused all of them to tear up as well and we, in that moment, realized that our bond was deeper than it has ever been. I've always been at peace with expressing emotions to them but I think we all feel that bond a little more deeply in this moment. By this point, I have found so many new areas of my power and I also realized that I don't want to do this alone but I will not yet ask them to become my proxy justice.

The Day is June the 18th, 2010 at 9:00 AM GMT

Today, we practice. The First Eye told me where to gather the scrolls, tomes, broken books, burnt papers, and other articles essential for my growth in this realm. I think I'm going to take some time away from this therapeutic journaling and devote my complete attention to this space in honor of the many minds that created this information.

The Day is June the 25th, 2010 at 9:00 AM GMT

Today, again, we practice and we begin. I will not be writing or recording but when I am ready to return here, I will.

The Day is August 2nd, 2010 at 9:00AM GMT

Today, I have 'remembered' an ability from long ago. I say remembered because I have become much better at channeling – this time I found the memory of an ancient priest that theorized timescale reflection philosophies. He calls it the expanded spatial observance theory. And I did it. I realize I can traverse the timeline as a memory observer; a passive viewer.

Yesterday, I developed my understanding of linguistics and I can now understand all languages from all peoples. The day before that I realized that I do not age but that the more separated from the scroll I became, the more it hurt. I need to find a better way to manage how to keep this as close to my skin as possible and at all times.

Much has happened since late June. My skin is void of all colors being only the hue of pitch black, my veins are always pulsing; shifting between neon crimson, electric blue, deep vibrant violet, and an energetic luminescent green. My eyes shift colors depending on which ritual and power realm I am calling upon, I am taller now – stretching from my initial height of 5'10" to 6'2", I have refused to get haircuts and only neaten up my ever-growing beard. I keep my hair in whatever hairstyle I am feeling in the moment but it is usually in a high-top with locs on the top and the left side of my head shaved – A fit that fits me well.

As I got up to take a break from some reading that I was doing I remembered that I still had the key that The First Eye gave me a few months back when I met him again on the street. I asked Dessen what it went to. Smiling, he told me to follow him and so I did. This castle is larger than any one person could ever truly explore and I would have never thought to look in this room within a room within a room. He took me to the top floor of the castle where we stood in an atrium. At the far end of the atrium was an ornate door that extended all of the way to the vaulted ceiling. He took out a blue and gold stone sphere from his necklace and placed it into the 'Grandauen Atrium Door.' After the door opened there were five additional doors in this hexagon-shaped room. Each of the walls were mirrors and the only distinction between them was a lock that took various devices to open. He went to the center door that was for the room called 'The Observer'len. It took a long key with radial spikes that looked like sun rays made of gold, and laced with shards of spirit quartz. He opened the door, and within that door was a room – within it was a closet. He asked me for the key I was given and I gave it to him. He placed the key within the door, took another key from around his neck and placed it into the other lock. He then turned to me and said, "This room is now yours, please." He reached out to dap me up as is our new custom and after that he walked through all of the doors, closing each as he continued back to whatever it was that he was doing before I asked him about this key.

I didn't hesitate after he left the rooms and I opened the closet. There was an incredible outfit inside and it was neatly separated by the type of clothing. There was jewelry, a short gold staff christened with spirit quartz and made of gold, all of the underlayers of clothing called anointed cloths, sandals, and a robe. I didn't' think anything would fit because well, how would it. None of this was mine initially and it wasn't tailored for me. I placed it on and noticed that I was a little correct on my fitting assumption. I wore it all downstairs and

Dessen told me that in the room that the outfit was in is a small scroll and that on it I must perform the scroll. I said to him, 'but the clothes don't quite fit right.' He said, 'you must trust that I will guide you properly here. I am the elder and one must honor the traditions from which we all hail, now please.' I slowly went upstairs being careful not to tarnish the articles of clothing I had dawned. When I got to the closet, I found that Dessen was right and that there was a small box with the scroll in it. I listened to my elder Dessen and performed it and that is when something incredible happened. The articles began to illuminate and conform to my body – I didn't know how I thought it would feel but I was quite surprised that it felt comfortable; it left me with a small semblance of ease. The only part I felt becoming more at ease than the overall clothing was the onyx box containing the scroll to my spine; it felt more protected. I don't know the extent to which I will suffer if it is ever separated from me but I knew it was the only thing I didn't see myself ever separating from or allowing anyone near given my experience with it in the hotel room.

I look at myself in the mirror as the castle's master clothier places the finishing touches on the clothes, I catch an ear of the local news. The reporter was talking about China's new interest in Africa and it reminded me of the second chapter of Chancellor Williams' book, 'The Destruction of the Black Civilization.' I know it's a different time but I couldn't help but to be a little taken by the fact that Africa has such wealth within her own borders but that other nations, itching for her treasure, find ways to always take advantage of her. Suddenly, a passing thought graces my forethought and I realize that I could do something about it. I could literally and immediately take a nation from any nation for my people as a healing space – that I could do so by any means I deem just and yet I am left wondering conversely whether or not this is actually just. Was this the choice that everyone around me seems to be inferring will be my decision alone to take?

A look of the truest levels of deep pensive thought have taken me and it is obvious. So obvious, in fact, that my friends ask if I am alright. I don't hold back from telling them a more expanded version of the choice I believe I am to make because sitting on the sidelines, either way, isn't an option.

I told them that I could take any nation from any nation, specifically the ones whose ethnic group caused harm on my people or invaded their lands and do with the inhabitants what I feel is just based upon the transgression. As they digested that portion and fixed their lips to say something, I continued to tell them the other side, that there could be another way to unify my people all across the still African nations of Africa and herald in a new age of prosperity and justice. Which option brings peace, which brings war, which is just; a deep debate occurs between us and eventually we are left with no true resolution. Both paths could be just depending on what realm of thought one is hailing from. It could be just to burn an eye for an eye and on the other end it could be equally as just to withdraw oneself from the sickness altogether and to heal amongst your own while protecting them the same. All of us have conflicting ideas and none of us a hardline stance on which option to take or when I should take it. The mood becomes melancholy and serious as we cautiously and pensively speak with each other on what is the noble path.

As I fall into the catacombs of my own thoughts, I look at my reflection in the mirrored glass. I begin to reflect that these clothes are more than clothes, these rooms are more than just rooms, these thoughts are more than just thoughts, these moments are more than just moments, I am more than just I. The deliberations we are having are a council meeting that will decide the fate of the world as we know it, for whichever path or paths we travel will have lasting ramifications on the ones we love, loathe, or feel neutral to the same. Whether I am reactive to the reality or proactive the same, one day some catalyst moment will happen and I hope that I won't be too old, too frail, too young, or too headstrong – instead – measured and just. As my friends continue the conversations, I break the cacophony of ideas by saying, 'We all have work to do. Whatever we do will be a jarring shift from the status quo that the world has known for too long. What we need to ensure is that we are all ready for the path we will choose, the path that will choose us, a combination of both, or neither – we need to prepare for anything. It's been a full day and it's time for every one of us to get some rest now. I love and cherish you all.' Without paying mind to whether anyone had additional thoughts I turned around, walked up stairs, removed my clothes and laid down. Before I fell asleep my Goddess came into the room, kissed me on the forehead, and we both drifted off to sleep together without saying a word.

The Day is August 3rd, 2010 – 11:43AM GMT

The news is back on the television as I walk downstairs to begin more practice and contemplation. There is an absolutely horrible story from back home in America. The shooting death of an unarmed black person in an apartment building where the officer entered into an apartment that she said she thought was hers. The part that infuriates me however, is not just the death of the black citizen just minding their own business in their own castle but that they chose to say he was under the influence of marijuana and that they chose a rosy picture of the officer that shot him. This is the sickness that makes me ever more sickened about the state of respect we Africans get no matter where we go. I wanted to feel the brother's final moments and so I sat on the floor and began the ritual to channel his spirit. I found the truth of their story and the truth of what happened there was that the officer knew him and killed him in cold blood – it could have been that they dated, it could have been rage, an argument – he isn't certain but whatever the case I felt sickened just as he did. He had his daughter in the next room and she was only twelve; reminding me of my own trauma the raging magma in my veins began to burn as if a cauldron of fire was pouring out of me. Scared for her life she hid in the closet until the scene became an official crime scene where she was found by crime scene investigative personnel. This breaks my heart. I am sorry I couldn't save this brother and so many like him. And I am sorry I have let down his daughter who will now grow up without him being there to guide her through her first days of high school, her first prom, her first driving test; through life.

In this moment, at this exact moment in the month of August, the day of the 3rd, in the year of 2010 at 12:06 PM GMT I will no longer sit idly on the sidelines while I have the will and I yield the power to do something about it. My training will accelerate now and I will help my people. Goddess, who is now standing behind me says, "I know what you are thinking my Love and I stand here with you to do it." She steps in front of me and says, "Do what you've been meant to do for a while now but be safe and don't let anyone else close. Find a sheath and be the idea that cannot be defeated and the man who doesn't exist." I thank her and walk off to peacefully channel The First Eye; I have questions.

The Day is August 6th, 2010 at 7:02 PM GMT

My works are known and I have done many things already. I have secretly stopped muggings; I have collected evidence of crimes against my people; I have done many things and these works feel good. I am still doing such work on a small scale and I need to find a better way to be more widespread with my responsibility. Crafting the recalibration of my people's spirit will take some time and a solid philosophy but how? Perhaps I should write a tome for it to be the will – there will be no 'perhaps', this is something I will do. But first, I need to take a walk through where my people are. I need to feel the balance, the grounding; I need to take a moment and truly observe from the ground gaining the back stories of the people living here and in the now.

I placed on my royal outfit and dawned my Shenarre. I then manipulated spatial time and traveled from my castle on the outskirts of Rome to Greenmount Avenue in Baltimore City, Maryland. It's about 11PM or so and as my journey for the day was concluding I came across a brother in the car sleeping and the police walking up on it with their guns drawn for some reason. I move closer and watch from the alleyway near the scene. The police yell commands at the brother in the car but he is clearly sleeping and unaware that they are about to turn him into another hashtag by bloodshed, fire, and rage. In practicing the honing of my abilities, I recalled a partially damaged scroll that was in my personal sanctum called, 'The Scroll for the Invocation of Kinetic Force Potential' created by an African ancestor priest by the name of Eiduren of the Easternmost Waters. The advanced portion of this particular scroll was badly damaged by fire after the temple in east Africa where it was held in was destroyed by invading Christian forces. I performed the ritual the first time but couldn't remember the invocation portion. I can hear the police yelling more commands at the brother as the situation becomes even more tense. I didn't struggle with the language as I know them all but the movements that accompany the rituals of the scrolls are sometimes hard to perform. I tried it again and failed on the same part but the third time I was able to call a barrier around the brother in the car. When police mistook him moving his hand to stretch, they fire a hail of bullets into the car. The bullets tear through the car as if the vehicle was paper being shot with a hundred shotguns; the glass on the vehicle shatters, the tires deflate, there is a thick smell of gun smoke that lingers in the crisp night air, and tensions are still high as the brother shockingly wakes up and steps out of the car looking at himself. This barrier of kinetic force potential is largely invisible and so he feels his chest, his arms, his legs. Surprised that he isn't dead or hit at all, he stands in shock as the police confusingly but just as angrily shout more commands at him. He is clearly stunned by not being dead, and so he moves his arms around franticly feeling his chest, legs, neck – everywhere, still shocked that he is alive. They attempt to tackle him to the ground since shooting him didn't work and that is when I became more frustrated. I stepped from the alleyway and yelled to them in a horrifically scary voice of power. "Watch your actions here against my people subject, for I will be swift in my deliverance of justice. If you do not change your ways, I will change your ways. Take this undeserved mercy as a series of final steps that will eventually break the camel's back." As I yelled, they turned their attention towards me and drew their guns in the same moment of time. I drew all of their guns into a red sphere I called in front of myself. I twisted the gun metal at my feet, lifted all of their vehicles and did the same, I caused the earth beneath us to rumble, began to levitate myself, and moved slightly forward in an aggressive stance to let them know, without saying a word, that I am not to be trifled with. I invoked a spatial state spell to teleport the brother over to where I was standing, formed the sigil symbol of my house and I traveled to another part of the city completely with Jessen. I told him to go home and to spend time with those important to him and to nay forget about what happened here; that his black life matters and that he should be more on-guard against any and all threats to it. I told him the words of the great black philosopher and activist, Stokely Carmichael, that, "If a white man wants to lynch me, that's his problem but if he has the power to lynch me then that's my problem." He is still in a state of shock but I could tell he had a question or two or ten. I told him to speak one question and he asked who I was before changing the scope to 'what' I was. I told him, "I am justice for you and all who look like you." I formed the same sigil symbol that I use to alter our spatial states in time, leaving to return to my home and I, in that moment, disappeared from his view. The Sennsen spatial state time ritual will be one of the most important rituals I have learned thus far. I can tell it will be a staple of my travel although it does extract a price. Perhaps I haven't quite mastered it yet, learned to control it, or perhaps that is just the cost of doing business with it. The First Eye once told me that the alteration of spatial states is among the most dangerous of rituals as shifting spiritual matter is one thing but physical matter is more densely bonded to the reality it is grounded to. He told me that our meat spaceship bodies don't take well to drastic change but that there were other scrolls to assist in mitigating the wear and tear on one's mind and body from using the spatial state ritual – It is a limited-spatial-state ritual that allows me to travel wherever on this Earth I must travel to within no true passing of time occurring. The First Eye told me that the longform version is the recommended one but that the short form could be used if needed in a hurry. The time difference between the two is pretty drastic considering the fact that I will likely be using this for on defense and offense but the chance for error in the short form admittedly leaves me scared. The repercussions of performing it incorrectly would lead to my spirit-body slipping into the chaos realm. I have linked the ritual to my sanctum sanctorum quarters and lined that entire area of my castle with all of the ritual books I have learned and those I have yet to master; many of them seem to share the same heritage as if they were a continuation of one unified work – how pleasantly African. I know a portion of black sandy residue is left behind after I perform Sennsen but I don't think it will be enough to cause any problems – my ignorance will likely get the best of me here but I will deal with that bridge if and when it comes – for now, it is time to rest.

The Day is August 7th, 2010 at 8:01 AM GMT

"Andrel, umm… Andrel you umm… yeah, you need to come down here like now bro." Derek yells from the main castle lobby. Thinking nothing of it I simply ask what the problem was – I assumed it was something related to something being broken or otherwise in the castle. He rewinds the news story that shows a rather frightening scene; one that I should have seen coming and prepared for accordingly.

Someone recorded a portion of my power showcase last night. It is obviously a cell phone recording – better than that, it was a few – /sarcasm. This story is being shown on multiple stations and all of them have the "Breaking News" banner with some questioning whether or not it was a hoax, deep fake, or a promo for some new movie – the police didn't help matters by being so closed-lipped and secretive about the occurrence.

One journalist at Politiology Sophos, seems to have her teeth sunk into finding the truth of this story. I know the Politiology Sophos and while they were once a hard-hitting voice of justice, they are now a shell of their former selves. Instead of bucking the trends and holding power accountable, they have become influenced by their insider status and the horrible way money influences the dissemination of information. What is real, what is important, what is void of either per editorial agendas and bottom lines – all of these and so much more are wrapped up in who is funding them at any given moment to report the angle the donors.

I found myself enthralled by their site, the initial article, and a particular reporter. She turned out to be a college senior and an intern at the publication. Apparently, this reporter has seen the sigil of my house before, and recalled some of the word I spoke although I was masked so she refers to me as an agent of the ancient collective. Her article is written for the public yes, but I can feel the words being driven at me.

My friends are more concerned at this point than at any other point before and Goddess is in tears. In their minds I could have died and well, they could be correct. I don't know the limits of this power and perhaps I should be more cautious with it until I do. A part of me is frustrated that I would even have to wait though – haven't our people done enough waiting for a helping hand? Haven't we been bamboozled into accepting everyone else's savior? Haven't we had enough of that foreign savior complex? How much longer should our people have to endure the struggle alone before I am really ready to help them? To be honest, just what the hell does ready even look like? Mentally pounding my own pensive head to dust I am becoming frustrated that I have all of this power but the resolve to really take advantage of it in service to my people.

As they talk louder at me and to each other, and as Goddess cries while trying to hold me I yell at them to just be quiet for a moment. I told them, I didn't have it in my mind to really search for a situation to place myself in but I was in the right place at the right time for the most horrible event that could have happened, I was there, and I did something about it. "I saved a brothers life you all! Doesn't that account for a certain level of risk?" I asked. They hesitantly agreed but it only made the sting of the situation's potential outcome less jarring. I made another attempt at reassuring them by telling them that I would be more cautious and use them as my immediate council.

I also told them that I would spend some time searching for this reporter who was searching for me. I know she has some questions and so do I – like how she knows certain things about my flow.

I ended up finding that her name is Grace Ariel Jefferson. I called her phone using an anonymous tip line she unofficially posted on her blog site and asked her about the progress she made on the case. After she began getting excited about her progress, I interrupted her and asked, "What if I knew where to find the one from that night?" She asked who I was and if we could meet and wouldn't let off of that. Believing I just made a huge mistake and that I'm possibly bringing her into unforeseen danger I hung up and decided to make certain she was safe instead.

I visited the local office myself and asked to speak to her on a story. I told them I was a source and that I could wait. She eventually came in and was accosted by her manager who in a confrontational tone told her, "Stop researching this story, quit asking about, drop the damn story. The police are already asking enough questions about it and we are not agitators to authority." She had a look of disgust in her eyes but begrudgingly said, "Yes sir, I'll follow up on the entertainment news story about cats and celebrities you put me on." She walked past me at first and then looked and said, "You're in my cube. Who are you waiting for?" I softly asked her if she found any residue from the person disappearing that night? Before she had a chance to answer I also asked her whether or not she was going to drop the story that easy. This particular question was partly a test to see how reticent she was to let the story go and also to see if she had the gall to continue with it despite the dangers to life, liberty, and financial stability it might cost. In the back of my mind I wanted her to be aggressive for the truth of who I was; the irony was that the person she is most looking for in this world is sitting right in front of her face.

Without answering the questions, she said, "I'm headed out for coffee, join me." It wasn't spoken as a request and I wasn't offended. I knew the context clue was that the office wasn't a wholesome place to talk about the story she clearly wasn't going to let go. At the local black-owned coffee shop about a block away, Urban Afro-Artisan Coffee & Creations Company, she told me she found a bystander that had a more in-depth video of the person in the alley before they put on the mask and that they got some of the dust in the alley before the police closed it off. She told me that the video, despite her best efforts didn't yield any results but that the residue came back from the lab. She said, "The lab said the substance wasn't completely from this world or anywhere on the periodic table for that matter." She elaborated, "I brought it to my manager who is my direct editor but he basically told me that this isn't the type of news they do here. He was like, we craft the minds of the American people through the type of news that keeps our bottom line healthy and whether you're employed here as an intern or not. He basically threatened my job here and was like, don't make waves here or you will never work in this industry again." She made repeated references to the findings by the laboratory where she sent the dust sample. They wanted to keep some of the powdery sand residue for further analysis but she insisted, and even went so far as to have legal threaten them with litigation if they leaked any information about it or kept any the same.

Grace also felt like it was straight crap that her manager was serving up on the threat so she told me how she planned to ignored it and keep pursing the story. I had half a mind to introduce her to my unofficial team. This was especially the case when she started bringing up information that only someone with knowledge of the scroll should know and I wanted to know how she knew, and even more so how much she knew.

It would appear that she knows there is something more special about it. In all honesty there is something special about it. It is a unique mixture of various earth elements comprised of powdered gold, amethyst and spirit-quartz grinded to a consistency of sand, as well as dehydrated and preserved lavender flowers, chamomile leaves, and lotus flowers they used to create it. They were all prepared four-thousand six-hundred and eighty years ago from today with each of the six ingredients being prepared in six individual parts of the African continent from the six founding members of the Council of Kerrhe.

At this point I felt like I could trust her. I cannot directly view people's ancestral lineage quite yet but when I physically touch someone, I can view their life memories as if I were in the movie theatre of their mind watching memory after memory, even if they don't recall it. I had an idea, I wanted to try something – just to really see if she can be trusted with coming more into the fold. I told her I could arrange a meeting with Andrel but after that she'd never see me again. I wanted to reinforce that she had one chance meet up with him. I explained to her that she had one hour to ask as many questions as she wanted. I asked, "What days aren't you available?" She replied, "Hmm… I'm pretty available this upcoming week but I do have a few things that are important on Monday." I smiled and said, "Well Monday it is then." With a confused look on her face she replied, "But I'm not free, didn't you hear me?" I smiled and said, "Yup, do you want your questions answered? Are you hungry for the truth? What are you willing to sacrifice in search of the answers that most plague you?" She didn't hesitate after that and agreed with a simple response, "I'm there like a hedge fund manager to a party with a room full of billionaires." When she agreed I told her the time and the place. I told her to meet me at the Library of The First Light, a public library that I own. I told her that when she walks in, speak to the librarian and ask for The First Eye. I explicitly told her, "When they ask, 'The First Eye, is that a book?' to reply, *'A book that is unwritten but rather the mind of light which owns it.'* She went to write it down and I told her, "No. You never write anything you are told from me or from the one you'll meet on Monday. You will memorize this, you will honor this, you will internalize this, you will devote yourself to it." I repeated it once more as she closed her eyes to force it to memory and then I told her, "I'm leaving." She stopped me from getting up by reaching out at the table; but I pulled back telling her, "I don't let people touch me, sorry but what do you need?" She asked, "The time, what time am I supposed to be there." I smiled and said, "Time is relative, figure it out." I wanted her to feel that she needed to be there from the time they open until the time they kick her out. I left the café and hopped in a cab, watching her watching me as she looked out of the window until we were both out of sight. I hope she doesn't let me down. I have a feeling she will search for this knowledge and dedicate herself to it. I could use someone like her on the team I am building.

The Day is Monday August 9th, 2010 at 7:02 AM

My public library opens soon. The library unlocks its main doors at 8:30 AM and I hired two people that don't know of each other from a millennial-style online classified search to watch the library for a certain person to enter it. I don't plan to show up there myself until after it closes and she gets kicked-out by the librarian. To my surprise, I am already receiving text updates from one of them to my anonymous number. It is only 7:50 AM now and one of them sees her. The other isn't there yet and that makes sense because I gave them an 8:10 AM call time. The person that sent me the text asked what they should do now and I simply replied to the message, "Just sit and watch for them to leave." They asked, "Is there a rear entrance she could leave out of? And why am I doing this?" I told them, "There is no rear entrance, and she is my sister. I am just making certain she is abiding by the terms of her trust fund is all. I'd like you to not ask any more questions other than that on the matter as it's a family thing and I would appreciate a little privacy. Thanks!" A text message arrived at 8:20 AM, "She is waiting outside on the steps looking at a book." Another message arrived at 8:29 AM when the library opened, "She was the first one in and I will let you know when she leaves." I let time pass as I spent the day doing other works relevant to my new life. Building an empire is something I slowly began learning how to do as I didn't want a second to go by in my life without progress being made in helping our people.

As the day drifted into the evening, I received another text stating, "It's 6:00 PM and she is walking out. Looks like the library is closed." I knew the library was closed as it's mine and I set the hours – I was already on the scene and as she was leaving, I waited for her to walk past an alleyway. When she looked down the alleyway, I made the same sigil symbol with my hands, illuminating the environment for a brief time. She recognized it and ran down the alley to see me. I was wearing the Shenarre, my ancient veil which sheaths my face from recognition. She angrily stated, "I've waited in there for you the whole damn day, didn't that guy that set this up know that? Didn't he know the location?" I am able to control the tones of my voice and the chorus of it when speaking. I allowed the full breadth of the ancestors to speak at once in a unified but calm tone. I told her, "I know you were there and even what time you arrived." I also proved as much by asking her, "On page fifty-two of the book you were reading called, 'Way of Light: The Expanded Volume', within paragraph four, in sentence three, what did you highlight?" She remembered it immediately and said, "Knowledge is laborious so seek the answers; enjoy the journey." Stunned by my voice and the fact that I knew exactly what she was doing, I told her, "Your hour of time with me hasn't started yet so don't worry. Before I share my answers with you, I need to know that your intentions are pure. When I touch your hand, I will travel down the path of your memories and witness what has brought you here." She said, "Brought me here today? Or in life?" To which I smiled and responded, "Time is relative." She placed her hand out and I held her hand while performing The Observer's Wayfarer Stone Ritual, which allows me to begin the observation of memories. This ritual also pauses time for everyone including me but only in a physical sense. It performs a stateful stasis; the Earth doesn't stop moving but instead my mind temporarily unlocks itself from the physical level of time and it is able to travel within the memories of someone else. I spent a few hours looking through her memories and when I let go of her hands only a few seconds passed. She asked if a few seconds was all I needed to which I said, "Time is relative; what was only a few seconds in passing was, for me, six hours." Before she had a moment to respond I told her, "Your hour of time begins now because you are true to your good intentions." She wasted no time at all and started off by noticing that after I made the sigil there was the same residue of sand left after it disappeared. She asked, "What is that sandy stuff that happens when you do that? Before I responded, she continued questioning me; it seems like regular elements but I know that there is something more so what is it?" I told her, "The 'sand' isn't actually sand but it is something called Jensagehn. The elements were brought forth from the six regions of Africa where the members of the Council of Kerrhe came from. The six elements you know of that are from this Earth are pure gold from the region of Syensar, Amethyst from the region of Duva, Spirit-Quartz from the region of Hehseni, Chamomile from the region of Partuk, Lavender from the region of Oolaehi, and Lotus flower petals from the region of Nihale. The other elements that, as your lab verified, are not from this world. Within each of the six ingredients I just gave to you remain a hidden chain of six sub-ingredients each containing six additional sub-ingredients six times over. What those are is not something however, I will share with you." She looked like a deer in headlights and looked down at her watch. She noticed twelve minutes had passed and immediately asked, "Who are you and where do you come from?" Right before I was about to answer she followed up in the same question with the addition, "And why are you here now?" I told her, "I would take it as one question. You may call me the Arbiter of Justice and, from a local and physical sense, I was born in Washington, DC. However, my spiritual connections stretch to languages, peoples, cultures, and blood that expand far beyond the locality of my physical and local being. I am here to be as my title states; I am the Arbiter of Justice and that is what you may see me as."

At this point, I see her looking around my Shenarre for any clue as to who I am – still curious even after I answered the questions from her. A part of me wants to let her know. I know she will never stop looking and at this point I know her intentions are pure but conversely, I know that I am relatively young in the scale of my powers and their scope. I, also, know what traditionally happens to young African-centered minds in this world; sharing such information with anyone outside of my small immediate council would likely result in my early retirement from such untapped potential – it is a risk I cannot take. I must be cautious slowly emerging from the cocoon that is my new path of growth.

She infers what Arbiter of Justice means and asks, "Can you elaborate on what you mean by Arbiter of Justice though?" I tell her, "You can report that the sightings of me are real and that I have been many places to intervene for the benefit and protection to life, liberty, and the pursuit of happiness of my people. You can report that I am the arbiter of justice, here for the protection of African peoples and I hail from the ancients of the motherland in unified totality."

She doesn't quite believe me I can see. I tell her, "Make certain your recorder can hear this part. I know you are recording it but I know your intentions are to privately study it to vet me as I have vetted you and this is fine. Call the Dallas, Texas police department and ask them about Case #3398549, then contact the Cleveland, Ohio police department and ask them about Case #95859474, finally, call the Santa Barbara, California police department and ask them about the person of interest from Case #573836335. I was the person of interest in all of these intervention acts whether they be attempted robberies, police violence; whatever, it doesn't matter I was there to defend my people." As I prepare to give her more cases to look into, she interrupts me and asks, "Can I conduct an exclusive interview with you then?" After thinking about it for a moment or two I agree because I have a feeling she can and will be an incredible unofficial public relations outlet for my mission here.

Before the on the spot interview begins, she tells me she plans to secretly launch it at the journalism publication where she works. She trembles lightly as she nervously stumbles over her words. Upon her face is a look of uncertainty and yet steadfastness; her eyes blinking rapidly as they dart around frantically searching for words that aren't there yet. I interrupted her and told her that she can certainly circulate the title, Arbiter of Justice as the short name. She seemed to find her mental footing and began paying close attention to my words. I told her that I however, have a truly different name; an actual name. I told her, "I am Enceri Otoyae Kharre, meaning, 'The One Bound to the Will of Justice's Justness." I painted a more artfully colorful version of my mission to protect the peoples of African descent worldwide. The whole interview, which was essentially me just speaking the questions I knew she would like to have answered for, took about fifteen minutes or so. After she stopped the recording, I shook her hand and this was the first time I took off my gloves to do so – I wanted her to see the color of my hands, temperature; the fact that it isn't completely, …human. Using the hand with no glove as the lead into the spatial-state ritual, the clarity of the symbols as the ritual is invoked is as clear as her attention was piercing. This ritual is usually an ebb and flow ritual with long stretches of slow form movements. It has only a few light jolts of the form towards the end as I manipulate the local fabric of spatial energy. I continued to perform the spatial-state ritual to completion and left her there, trusting that she could follow the many breadcrumbs I gave to her during the interview. I am quite happy with who she is so I don't have any doubt she will proceed to help me in my mission here.

Upon reaching my home state again, I realized just how tired I was after I nearly stumbled through the spatial-state ritual; it was the first time I had ever felt disjointed from my local reality. It seems dangerous to partake in this ritual when I am depleted of my energy – the feeling is akin to swimming from one end of a small pool to another versus fighting a current in all directions while attempting to swim across an ocean of chaos. I decided to take the rest of the day and rest lest I succumb to the chaos realm brought forth by improper form.

The Day is August the 10th, 2010 at 10:08 AM

I've been up for a little while now. I feel quite rested and so I thought it best to get some scrollwork completed. Today, I was working on a ritual of environmental transmutation called, Ritre Enegem by a female priest of architectural harmony and balance from the southern portion of Africa. I haven't yet been able to master this one; it is quite difficult and requires an incredible amount of mental balance as you are building structures at a molecular level and bending them to your will without touching them. It follows a skill tree of scrollwork that is a branch from the spatial-state ritual; it is dramatically more difficult to control the chaos forces of the natural world. However, mastering this scroll will allow me access and some semblance of control over the chaos realm, which the Kerrhian Priestesses call Xenelles Vargelles.

Suddenly Ashley yells for everyone to come look at what is going viral all over the internet. I heard her yell but I was sluggish for two reasons – I kind of knew it was likely the news story and I was also kind of busy with the Ritre Enegem. As the rest of my friends and my Goddess saw it, they pretty much compelled me to meet them downstairs in the Reflection Room of the main castle. Grace, published the story already. It was a full-blown written piece, complete with video, audio, and external links. The title of the piece was, "Black People Rejoice: The Arbiter of YOUR Justice is Here" and the sub-title was, "An Exclusive Interview with The Enigmatic Arbiter Himself." My friends and my Goddess wanted to talk about it; I could tell they were slightly upset, partially fearful, and marginally happy so I want to honor their feelings as my council but I told them I have to do something for a little while and that I'd be back soon. I changed clothes and used the ritual of spatial state again to get myself close enough to her office whereby I walked in and asked to see her. The receptionist was busy and only half-paying attention to me, so I escorted myself to her desk where I saw some of her colleagues approaching her for violating company policy. They were quite upset that she released this work under her company's banner without approval. A taller gentleman was visibly showing contempt, utter anger, and resentment for her actions. He wasn't of African descent and based on his comments, didn't care much for doing those stories anyway even if it were written about his own culture. I stood up and was about to speak to her honor by acting like a member of the public that was so happy to hear about that level of journalism but then a person walked in from the elevators nearby where I was sitting and the floor fell silent. He told Grace, in front of everyone on the floor, "I am so proud of what you have brought to us. You could have taken this anywhere. You could have given up on the story – I know this couldn't have been easy to gather and even harder to push through our filters. I am proud of you for opening my eyes to just how fulfilling it is to be a journalist again. I woke up this morning with my phone going crazy from other journalist, our public relations department; my mother and father in the United States." He continued, "It is ironic that at one point I was the young one bucking the trend and teaching my parents, the world, and my closest peers – hell, it's how I got here in the first place. How fitting is it that you have just done the same and you know nothing about the world – such youthful fire and innocence. The money it takes to run this place would make your head spin and the amount of sucking up we have to do for funding and access would make your head spin even more. Perhaps, we should tune a large section of our senses back to respecting the bullish nature of youth in proper form – perhaps, we should return to being the cultured bull through the china shop of corruption and we are accountable – that, we should root out corruption and let the people know no matter the cost. Hmm…" A look of contemplation and excitement is visible on his face now. He turns to the floor manager and says, "I'm hiring her. Build her a team of people, if any, from this floor she wants to lead and I will take care of the rest. I am going to get her the protection she will need. Equally, I want all of you to decide what kind of journalist you want to be because we have a new vision that will be full "Grace" and if that isn't you then may the force be with you as you get your hell out of my office." He walks off to do whatever it is he is inspired to do because of Grace. She brought life back into this organization by simply sacrificing herself in pursuit of the knowledge and the dissemination of it. I left as everyone was still in shock but applauding her – no one really paid attention to me coming in or leaving out which is exactly how I want to maintain my presence.

Talking with my friends and Goddess, I can tell they are not too pleased with my methods; they must've had time together to really hash it out before I got there. They state their objections and concerns and to be honest they are valid. I let them know that I am taking it all into account as I prepare myself more for the mission that I have the responsibility of executing. As the conversation softened, I officially told them about some ideas I had been quietly contemplating and where I wanted them to fit in, should they elect to stay with me on this path. I told them that The First Eye collected fourteen castle estates across the world and that I wanted them to manage their power as regional justices. They all went silent. The only person that knew I would do something like this was Goddess as I had already pretty much told her without telling her during one or ten or so of our many times together recently. I divided the world into specific regions that included bodies of water and showed my friends the two regions I wanted them to manage. I turned towards Derek and Shanice. I told them, "Derek and Shanice, I want you to perform duties on my behalf as my Left Tenant Regional Justices; executing will with the full powers of the regional assets." I looked at Omar and Ashley. I told them, And I want you both, Ashley and Omar to perform duties on my behalf as my Right Tenant Regional Justices; executing will with the full powers of the regional assets." I told them all, "You shall be co-rulers and perform works that benefit our people."

As I held my Goddess' hand, I told her something she didn't even expect. I knelt down and proposed to her. I wanted her to be my co-ruler, The First Goddess of Justice. I told her, "Without you, my Goddess, I would have broken down beyond repair a thousand times over. I was a puzzle, made of a thousand-thousand pieces, and missing pieces. There have been many times now that I have come to understand why our ancient ancestors realized that feminine and masculine energies work best when they work in tandem, so too have I realized that without you I cannot be truly effective in this role or any role the same. I would be honored if you would become The First Goddess of Justice and execute whatever will is just in your eyes." Before she could even say yes, she started to cry, then Ashley held her hands to her mouth and cried, and then Omar, Shanice, and Derek did the same. She composed herself just enough to say yes. Omar went to get the ring that he kept with him throughout the entire trip. I placed it on her finger and the mood was in complete exacerbated jubilance. We all lived in the greatness of that moment — the moment that all of us became uniquely elevated to new milestone levels in our life paths that weren't initially accessible. Well into the evening hours we sat in the room of the castle dedicated to global planning. The First Eye called that room, The Architects Constellation and I loved the name so I carried it on but appended the word 'council' to the end. We were brought food from the kitchen for lunch and dinner and it wasn't until dinner that I realized all of my friends were now also eating a vegan diet. I asked what caused them to begin their transition and they told me that they had been reading much of the material in the nutrition, and spiritual wellness areas of the Grand Apperception Library; a masterfully built smooth stone ten-story building with a luminous sparkling gold between the stones as mortar. It must've been during the times I was practicing, in my own head, doing other works, out and about or resting but I was proud. I asked them, "How deep are you down the rabbit hole of more than local awareness of the sum of one?" Shanice spoke for them all and said, "Between all four of us, fifteen books have been started, seven completed, and we have been cross-briefing each other on the knowledge. Beyond that we've been researching mindfulness, harmony, law, justice, and my own personal favorite the migrations of ethnic groups across the span of recorded human history." Ashley added, "Not to be blunt but we considered ourselves as your council long before you officially asked. We are family and we didn't want you to have this burden alone so we told ourselves that we would pour ourselves into self-betterment, awareness, and high-culture knowledge." I was so impressed that I just said our usual chill phrase, "Clutch of the MVP", which pretty much means 'that's the best of the best; cool.' We all ate the rest of our dinner together, laughed, bonded, shared more stories from recent adventures, and then around ten PM'ish we went off to bed. Goddess and I decided to walk the castle grounds as we looked at the moon, held hands, and silently reflected on the great milestones and challenges we have taken on from the beginning of whence we came to where we stand now.

The Day is August the 11th, 2010 at 5:04 AM

I'm up pretty early today but I don't feel tired. I'm likely still pretty high-inspired from the past couple of days as there has been great progress made with much great work left to do. I smelled coffee as I walked down the stairs. I love the fact that we source our own coffee from one of the seventeen farms we acquired in Africa. Smells like an Ethiopian blend today and that's one of my favorites – ah, the day will be good. As I walked down the stairs, I began to hear people talking. To my surprise everyone was up and working on plans at the table, per their new paths in life. I grabbed a cup of coffee and with a tone of happiness said, "So what's the occasion?" They told me to pretty much sit down and hear these great ideas they had for their regions. They showed a plan for setting up special schools and within new communities they would build. They had entire plans for sub-cities that they wanted to make; complete with their own grocery stores, banks, nurseries, spiritual centers, a citizen council building, museums, and other great articles. One of the cool things they designed was uniqueness amongst them in the products and services they would specialize in. One of the sub-cities was to be known for being the masters of metalworks, another being the masters of the traditional arts, with another being known as the masters of agriculture, and so on. What was so impressive is that they would share agreements with each other for buying and selling materials to one another. There were so many great ideas within this model and I sort of interrupted them and asked them what they were calling this project. They told me that it didn't have an official name but that the working project name was 'Operation Community Afro-Silk Type

Thing.' They asked for my permission and that's when I let them know that they didn't need it. I told them that I trusted them to work autonomously without micromanagement or approval. These were people I grew up with and trusted one-hundred percent with the management and execution of our noble mission. Without hesitation they went off to begin their works. I commissioned a central region castle be erected for my Left Tenant Regional Justice and another for my Right Tenant Regional Justice. I also commissioned a motorcade for each of them along with all necessary preparations for general castle administrative operation. I let them select their own staff and placed their hiring process through the strict lens of my castles staff; we must be certain who we hire are honorable and truthful in their intentions, especially given the volume of benefits we offer and the unique mission we are charging them to support. All of this work is slated to be complete by June 1st, 2011 and this includes the new building for my Goddess and I in the District of Columbia. This castle in Rome is my Right Tenant jump point and the District of Columbia castle is my Left Tenant jump point. Our plans are all in motion and until then we will train, build on the plans more, and I, specifically, will become a master of my duties. I will spend the duration of time between now and June the 1st, 2011 between the Grand Apperception Library and my Sanctum Cocoon mastering every scroll, strengthening every connection, and progressing through the three-hundred and sixty degrees of each of the three-hundred and sixty constellations, per the learning path The First Eye told me about. I will not be writing here during that time; this work will take my full dedication, consistency, and every ounce of spare attention I can muster. I'll be in hermit mode before my full-fledged public first homecoming.

The Day is June the 3rd, 2011 at 8:10 AM EST

I am in the Left Tenant Castle of the Justice Apperception, commissioned as 'Riseneya.' Riseneya is a magnificent ten-acre property in Washington, DC located in the Northwest section of the city. It is a collection of seven buildings with a connection building in the center. All of the buildings are individual but they are connected by a semi-open walkway system between them. They are equally spaced from each other and the central gate yields to an ornate visitor center before you enter the main grounds. This castle isn't open to the public but for guests, events, etcetera having the option to allow large groups of my people in was essential. There are two libraries on this campus, my living quarters, a museum and art gallery, an ancestral worship temple, a nursery building, and the 'Buildings of Fountains.' I am pleased with how this came together and it always feels good seeing the amount of respect we receive when leaving the complex in our motorcade, even though no one really knows who is in the vehicles. Our schools are performing well, the communities are beginning to come together wonderfully, and the amount of monetary power that we are instituting in our people is impressive considering the fact that our works are less than a year old. I decide to travel amongst our works and the areas that we have not yet seen progress outside of their sphere; admittedly however, there have been clouds darkening with respect to hostility towards us. There have also been moments where I have been a witness to some slave-state mentalities within our people. There was a quote I recalled from long ago that stated, "Black unity starts with saying hello." I noticed however, when visiting some of the large cities that there was quite a bit of negativity lingering in our people. I know that much of this comes from environmental conditions, or at least that's what I'd like to believe. I have not let anyone, even my council, see the new abilities and strengths I have – let alone the world at-large has no idea I even exist outside of Grace doing her job letting people know there is an Arbiter of Justice out there somewhere. I suppose it didn't help that I locked myself away for nearly a year while I mastered my given abilities. I should give her a call – better yet, I'll make a visit.

I decided not to spatial state travel this time and I asked Goddess if I could take her private plane to Rome to check-in on Grace at the journalism outlet. I told her that I wanted to also see about more officially bringing her on as our direct public relations person if and when we get to that level of outreach. Goddess was for it and so off I went. I was excited to share our works with Grace. I landed in Rome, and arranged for the Right Tenant Castle of the Justice motorcade to pick me up. I arrived at the publication in my Shenarre, walked into the building and asked for Grace. It was in this moment that I was presented with the most heartbreaking news that would end up being a string of bad news I would receive. The main receptionist in the lobby just looked down with a face of sadness and called for someone named Thomas to meet me in the lobby. I thought it would be the case that she simply quit or was poached by another company, or even perhaps that she started her own but I was completely wrong. She went missing a few weeks earlier and was found a week ago in a dumpster. Her body was mutilated, she was tortured, shot, and she had a noose around her neck. Thomas, that name should have rung a bell as she mentioned him twice before; they were just married and he decided to take on her work after her death in her honor. He told me she tried to reach me but didn't know how – she didn't feel safe doing the work she was doing. I realized; I didn't leave her with any number and my team didn't really think to check in on her as we were expanding – a horrible oversight that obviously we cannot afford after such a fate. I was so grief stricken that I decided to stay there and perform works myself in her honor. The murder was also unsolved and I wanted to personally handle that case. They already buried her so I couldn't try touching her hand to see her memories again – I'm not even certain it works on those who have passed on. Just then, the police entered the building and attempted to apprehend me. I realized they were looking for me before but it has been almost a year and I haven't been anywhere doing anything. I was already in such grief and horribly upset that her killers weren't caught by the justice of the government whose jurisdiction she was within. I was even more upset that here they were accosting me about the non-violent works I performed in service of the life of my people. Grace died because of me and I couldn't contain my rage and, in that moment, my hatred. I looked outside and saw that police vehicles surrounded my motorcade which made me even more furious; I felt my veins beginning to burn underneath my clothes. This is petty work and I can easily get around it – I don't have the patience or composure for this today. I told the journalism company that I would be back and that I would personally handle the protection of the team carrying on Grace's work. The police who are still yelling at me to put my hands up and come with them are but peons to my potential so I continue ignoring them as I told Thomas to prepare his team and all of the work. I told him to tell the founder to call the number of my Master at Arms for the Right Tenant Castle of the Justice; that all would be handled through that channel. In that moment, the police attempted to apprehend me as I was closing out my conversation with Thomas and I pushed him clear across the room with a mere fling of my wrist. Another officer deployed his taser on me and I let it hit me. As the voltage coursed through my body, attempting to subdue me I slowly lifted my hands to remove the Shenarre. No one has seen my face in public without it and even more so since the changes from additions in my power state – only Goddess has seen the fullest me. Upon seeing my face, my skin, my eyes – and after seeing my powers in the flesh there was a visible stench of fear in the room from the authorities. I spoke with a voice of ferocity, "I am practicing an incredible volume of restraint as I stand before you with an incredulous disposition. I could dismantle you and all you know within a simple wish of it to be so and yet I allow you to place your violent intentions on me! You cannot harm me and so I fling you from my sphere of attention as if you were a fly to a dinosaur do you understand? I am the law now and there is no amount of firepower you can hail against me to change this." The officers were visibly shaken but still proceeded to apprehend me so I expressed another passive power by lifting the officers and moving them out of the building, removing them from surrounding my vehicles. I walked outside to a large crowd of bystanders, I turned to them and said, "A noble journalist here was murdered in cold blood by cowardly actors and instead of utilizing all resources to solving that crime, your authorities want to apprehend me. I will not allow it any longer. How many ills against African people has this Catholic city committed? How many ills has this world done to African people? Where is the recourse? Where is the cessation of aggression against African people? Grace Ariel Jefferson has told you about my works. I haven't harmed anyone and yet I am being apprehended. Who will apprehend the corrupt actors that mold justice to their compromised whims? I cannot be shaken, and I will not be silenced. I am the Arbiter of Justice and it will be done. Whomever it was that facilitated the murder of Grace, know this – I will exact justice on you. To all others that have negative intent against African people, against my African people, I will exact justice on you. No one will stop that mission. My people will rise to their due level of reverence on this planet – I swear it." There are cellphones out and those who aren't recording are in shock at what they are bearing witness to. I touch each of my vehicles and use a ritual of matter spatial state manipulation to send them back to the Right Tenant Castle of the Justice, called Lexseghn. I also moved myself to my sanctum jump point in Lexseghn.

I'm pacing in Lexseghn right now I'm so grief-stricken and enraged. The world knows my name now. They don't know my place of residence and none of the vehicles have traceable license plates – they route to an infinite web of other points. I know for a fact now that my people will never know peace unless we have a place to know peace – a place we manage, that is just for us, with us, created by us as it was in the beginning. I personally looked up the cemetery where Grace was buried and used the spatial state ritual in order to shift myself there. I mastered the ritual of matter manipulation a while ago and called upon it to neatly rise her casket from the ground. Filled with inconsolable pain and a low-resistance to peace should I find out who was involved in the murder; I haven't felt such grief since the visions of the pain of our ancestors kept showing me their memories. I know I should have asked Thomas before doing this but these are extreme circumstances and I want to know who the hell killed my friend and I cannot see myself pausing that for anyone; I feel I am at fault and this is the justice I owe to Grace, although I don't know what I'm going to do when I find those responsible for this. Her casket now lay in front of me and I am attempting to suppress the anger that will certainly crash into my peace-centered state; if I see the noose marks, the gunshots, the stab wounds, the burns; any of it – I think I might lose all composure. But alas, this needs to be done – I owe it to Grace. After a few moments I finally compose myself enough to open her casket. As soon as I saw what they did to her, I broke down into tears and apologized to her for what I got her into. I went to touch her hand and nothing happened which made me feel even worse than I had already felt about doing this. The ritual doesn't work on material components lacking the spirit-matter after such passing of time and that has now been proven to be the case. I close the casket and sit by it on the ground in despair with my head hanging. At that moment I decided to talk to someone who I have a feeling might be able to help. I channeled The First Eye and asked him, "How do you deal with such anger and grief when you have the power to enforce whatever ends you deem righteous? Is it even right to seek just vengeance against ill actors? What am I supposed to do here?" The First Eye told me, "You know that you can channel Grace, right? But before you travel down that path, I strongly suggest you find balance in your own self. I cannot even begin to understand how hard of a choice it is you are now being committed to make. You are absolutely justice for our people and that comes with many areas of responsibility. The Council of Kerrhe has left a few tomes on the subject of how they intended for it to be but I was not able to acquire those. They are held in the Vatican's private collection of artifacts. I know you are able to get there with people seeing you or without the same but the decision on what route to take is up to you. As it relates to Grace and what to do; ask her and walk forward from there."

I sat in the correct position to channel someone other than The First Eye. As I phased into the spiritual realms of immaterial beings, I called into the light for Grace to conclave with me. As if she was waiting, she appeared as a being of light. I told her how sorry I was for what had happened to her and that I felt like it was my fault for putting her in this position without properly protecting her. She stopped me and said, "I knew what I was getting into and I would have eventually found my way to an early end whether I found you or not. You know this path is dangerous for our people, especially the ones who don't have the abilities you do while they are living. The world at-large has taken that school from us and has housed it away in the deepest annals of their power centers. I know you are seeking vengeance for those who murdered me and to be honest it is justified.

Your role, Mudlahsee is to be the arbiter of the will of justices' justness; so, do it. Find them and bring them to justice." She reached out her hand so that I could see her memories and I first asked her, "What is the justice that should be delivered though? I don't know what I am supposed to do on that front and I don't have the books of guidance. The rage in me wants to just obliterate them and all who support, endorse, abed, and finance this same mindset. But is that justice?" Grace responded, "I know you have tried to channel the Council of Kerrhe but as you know they made an ultimate sacrifice. There were only six council members and the sacrifice was that they were cast into stasis with their powers being bound to the scroll they left behind. They cannot yet converse, interact, or conclave with anyone outside of themselves; this includes the spirit realm. They locked all of their power, wisdom, ritual book locations, and so much more within the scroll that gifted you your abilities. What they defined as justice was never truly defined. I believe they intended for you to find your own way in whatever time period it is. I hope that helps, now touch my hand and take my memories with you." I hesitantly touched her hand and saw the seven people that committed the act along with the four people that allowed it to be so and I became furious. My blood felt like rivers of unstoppable magma all over again. I'm going to end them; I am literally going to rip their souls apart. I left the spiritual realm, stood up, placed her casket back, and decided that I will be public, I will protect my people, I will find and deal with her murderers publicly, and nothing we do will be stopped, confronted, questioned, or likewise; our mission is simple – protect our people from the pain of any one person or people, intending to cause harm to us, period.

I shifted to the first murder's home while he wasn't there. He is a father who loves baseball; there are posters, bats, baseballs, and other artifacts all around the garage. He enjoys the beer brewing culture; there are empty ornate kegs and brewing gear around. He is a circuit court judge; his law degrees are proudly displayed in the office of his home. His political ideology is right leaning; there are party pamphlets everywhere and on this car in the garage there are bumper stickers. One would think he is a decent person but all too often the most racist members of society hide beneath the veil of tact and gentle intentions. He has a family and I feel the best justice I can gift to Grace is to expose this horrible person; to rip his soul from his body and to tear it apart so that it may never know peace. I saw in Grace's memories that he was wearing a mask that he threw away and that he was the one responsible for stabbing her in the face, neck, and in her groin; the knife he used has his DNA all over it and he foolishly kept it as a token of pride. As I looked more into his life I was again conflicted, I should just kill this asshole and be done with it; an eye for an eye. Just then I had a great idea; I would establish my own system of justice and take actions against anyone that performed violent acts against my people – that I would let a panel of my people decide what recourse is just. Yes, that would send a grand message to every one of every nation that I am here to root out the ill members of society in honor of my people. I will call this panel of justice, The Blackened Wolf Pack – I will collect the evidence and deliver it to my people along with my testimony and we will exact justice from there. But this asshole will get no panel. He will receive my personal gift of deliverance. I shifted to the courthouse where he works; the guards at the door didn't attempt to stop me – they looked like brothers and sisters of the diaspora and I felt that they knew I was here for a just reason. I walked up the stairs as the citizens began screaming, recording me, and running to get away. I shifted to the floor where the Judge Alitta was presiding over cases and as I stood in front of the door, I heard a flurry of sirens coming from outside – looks like the police and the military are here now. When will they learn their lesson? Today, I will teach it to them. I blew the door open with a blast of purple fire and as the wood burned ferociously in the courtroom the citizens ran from the door around me. I told Judge Alitta, "I know you had a hand in killing Grace Ariel Jefferson and now I will deliver justice in the name of Grace and of all my people." I physically grabbed him by the neck and dragged him outside, slowly, and taking the long route; my hand burning the back of his neck. As we got to the front doors, I threw him outside with a violent push through the glass doors. As he laid there unable to move, I confronted the police and the military. I said, "You all insist on pushing me to the edge of resistance to violence; you beg for me to obliterate my restraint." As if much of them were ignoring me they drew their weapons and demanded I stopped my actions. I simply said no and decided that I would, in that moment, show them their error. I raised my arms to the sky; it grew dark with rolling thunder piercing the wind. I formed 'The Ritual of Ashes'; walking towards the bottom of the stairs as I performed it. It began to rain; black rain drops pierced the air and purple lightning struck all around us damaging the tops of buildings nearby. My staff turned from its short gold posture to a gold staff with purple lightning protruding from both ends. I effortlessly pulled the helicopter above to me; the pilots and police shaking with fear in their eyes and frantically trying to resist – feeble. I flung them from the helicopter and proceeded to turn it to ashes at my feet, then I walked forward. I grabbed the militarized vehicles to my left and right and struck them with lightning that turned them to ash. By this point, the police and military foolishly started to shoot and so as if the bullets were air passing my face, I turned the bullets, the guns, the rest of the cars, all of it became ash at my feet. I rose Judge Alitta and said, "It's over." I continued as I rose him high into the sky. In the view of the crowd, I loudly said, "Your racism is a sickness that has caused horror to many lives across many generations; generations where my people suffered at the hands of yours. You stand here as a Judge, within your institution, sickening it with the motives of your evil. Wherever you and your kind hide I will find you and they will face the horror that I am; I will rip your soul from your body and burn it with the flames of my people's pain." I grabbed his spirit by the neck, and dragged it out of him as he screamed in agonizing pain. When his body fell limp to the ground it turned into ashes. I held his spirit-body within my hands and I followed through on my justice, ripping his soul apart; that he will know no rest but will instead spend countless eternities in countless realities – unable to collect his memories and transition. This was my first mortal kill and while it didn't feel good, it had to be done. There is no prison for people like this; I am the pain of my ancestors and sometimes from that pain justified rage comes to the surface. I will burn the souls of the remaining six and of whatever numbers across this world sympathize with violent terroristic racism.

One of the murderers was a police lieutenant, two were construction works, one was a teacher, and the remaining two were members of a motorcycle club. I obliterated their spirits in a similar public fashion to reinforce that I am the recourse for the violent expression of ideas against my people. However, I feel drained. This was not an easy day, nor was it one I was looking forward to – I tried so hard to avoid this day but I keep being pushed towards a hard decision that I am not ready to make. I shifted back to Lexseghn where I was met with my people in a saddened awe. They saw it on my face that what I was forced to do hurt me deeply. Before I went into the silent space of my sanctum sanctorum, I left them with a charge.

I instructed the Lexseghn staff to work with the Riseneya staff to quickly establish The Blackened Wolf Pack. I didn't want to have to become the violence that the world has forced upon my people if I didn't have to. They wasted no time as much of the framework for such a force was already in play. We had recently established our own private armed forces called the Nelhenar. As they procured established judges and citizen committees for the deliverance of justice, the Nelhenar went to collect the evidence using similar tools and functions that the governments of the world utilize. Calmer and yet still grief stricken I turned my attention to the theater of Riseneya. I called upon my Left Tenants, my Right Tenants, and my Goddess to join me – they, at this point and from doing their own works, agreed without hesitation that this was a reasonable step forward.

I shifted back to Riseneya and took my royal motorcade to the gates of the White House in Washington, DC. I got out of the car in my Shenarre and as people looked when the authorities confronted us, I removed the Shenarre so all could see my face. As the tourists took pictures, the police drew their weapons, and the mood turned from peaceful to tense I made my first public declaration. My proxy justices were on my flanks and Goddess was there as well. I shielded them with a protective veil as they stood silently beside me. I slowly removed my royal robes so that the world could see the full depth of my skin. It pulses with red veins. There are random stripes of white that form symbols across my chest and there are lines of purple that stretch vertically from my shoulders and flow down my back. There are green flashes across my rib cage that pulse at random intervals and the eyes of the crowd cannot believe what they are bearing witness to. I called upon our space darkened clouds with purple lightning flashes in the sky. I called upon our space the black rain drops that mirrored the consistency of blood but were as black as tar. I wanted them, nay, I wanted the world to see that I had the power to show up uninvited to a great seat of perceived power. I began to levitate myself over to the gates as my proxies stood still at the front gates in their respective regal outfits. As I got to the gates the guards, with fear in their voices told me to stand back as they will use lethal force. Their basic firepower weapons are as effective as cutting down a tree with a plastic spoon and I let them know as much as I moved their cars, took their guns, and forced them face down on the street. I walked past them and walked through the closed iron entrance gates. As I walked over the lawns, I went to the spot where the situation room was and I made a public showing of power again. I could have simply shifted to the Situation Room but instead I tore the ground apart and raised the entire bunker, without destroying the White House itself. After the bunker rose, I let it drop to the ground as to make a thud but to not harm anyone and then I tore open the concrete and steel to expose all of those inside. The cameras, I am certain see that it is the President surrounded by his staff and security. This is when I told him, "You think you are in control. You control nothing when our black minds realize our history. You control nothing but the artificial machine of institutional racism, classism, and sexism that bull-dozes over the lives and freedom of my people but it ends today. I am justice and no thing, and no one will stand in its way. There is no higher court of decision than me. Your military can swarm and you can attempt to fall back on your paper laws but I am not here to waddle in the institutions that have held us back. Our people have our own and we will return to them whether you like it or not. This showcase of power that I have brought directly to you is meant to serve as a warning that I will come for you directly if any harm comes to my people from the hands of outside cultures." The President just stood silent with a look of fear and confusion on his face as I continued. I looked at his aides and said, "Record this and heed its time schedule. You have exactly seven cycles of the Sun to arrange an emergency session so that I may brief the world. I don't have to rely on you to get this done but I am again attempting to work out a greater peace for my people without falling back to what you and your ancestors have always done to get your will; conquest, conquer, kill, and control. If you miss this time schedule however, what I do next will be completely on you." I moved all of the disturbed Earth and placed his bunker back down where it once was, restoring all of the damage as if it never happened. As I stood on the lawn and the final tree was reestablished in its original spot I walked back to where my proxies were standing. We all got in our vehicles and they drove us back to Riseneya. As we drove away and Goddess looked out of the window, I reflected on the fact that I still don't quite know what decision I will eventually make. I can take any nation, all nations, or whatever for the benefit of my people and do with the current inhabitants whatever I wish or I could attempt to use these power tactics to gain respect without executing mass upheaval. In any case, my decision today will change everything or it will change nothing; I certainly hope for the former so I won't have to deal with where this world will force me to go if it is the latter.

The Day is now June the 6th, 2011 at 8:01 AM

I was alerted that we had our time and date on the world stage. I was ready for this moment. I have the world stage for as long as I want it and the coordinators, a large four-hundred-member group of planners, wanted to know where the event will be held. I had already prepared Riseneya for the event so that is where I decided it will take place. It will occur out in the open in the amphitheater just next to my main living quarters. I set the date for June the 26th, 2011 at 9:00 PM EST and just like that the wheels were in motion. My Master at Arms for Riseneya Castle told me that there has been a large influx of applications for people wanting to work at Riseneya. I was happy to hear that but then he added, many of them are not Africans or African children of the diaspora. He asked, "What should we do about this? What is your directive on this?" It didn't take me too long to come up with my stance. I told him, "Other ethnic groups can be allies if they wish to assist in rooting out racism wherever it lives and such but they cannot work, live, or function within our centers themselves. I do not feel it is just to so actively work to build a national community of peace and healing for my people if we allow other ethnic groups to join our ranks. It is not a 'negative' mark against them but rather a stance that we must take in order to heal and build ourselves without the active assistance of others at this time." I paused for a moment and told him, "Contact Thomas Jamison, our new Media Director and have him draw that up for public release. Also have our Human Resources Director make my wishes into policy. I'd like to continue focusing on my speech." Djosen, the Master at Arms for Riseneya was relieved to hear that I believe. I could tell by the lowering tension stress in his shoulders that he wanted this to be my response and reasoning; I am happy I didn't disappoint. I decided to appoint a Minister of the Will of Justice to hold meetings with castle directors on various matters and to handle them accordingly while coordinating with the Minister of the Will of Justice at the sister castle.

The Day is now June the 7th, 2011 at 7:02 AM

I barely find myself with enough lethargy to want to go to sleep these days. In fact, Goddess and my other proxies are all in the same boat. We realized it as we all had breakfast together this morning. There was a noticeable silence but smiles all around the table as we all reflected for a short moment on how far we've come, how young we are; the jittering ideas of what to do next are a constant – so much so that we set up a board for ideas to be showcased. Our lives are pretty much all over the place now as people know our real names, our family's names; so much has changed in the short span of what feels like but an hour or so. All of our more immediate families have been given protection by our Nelhenar if they wanted it or have moved onto the guest houses at any one of the various castle complexes. Things do seem just a tad bit tense outside as we prepare for our true first homecoming – I ordered radio silence across all of our communities from a government perspective and so speculation has been running rampant. Some news stations across the world are labeling us as liberators, others terrorists, others are reserving judgement. But the one thing that is pretty interesting across all of public discourse is hailing from the viewpoints of the various ethnic groupings and cultures. Some are highly supportive, some critical, some communities look like us and others not so much. No matter the viewpoint however, it is really nice to see such vibrant discussion on the history of the world. People are really taking this Arbiter of Justice title to heart and paying reverence to the fact that the world has done wrong by black people for thousands of years. All of the world's media has become as vibrant in discussion and higher-thought just as Grace had done.

Constant news stories on every station and internet platform, journalists of all types, law enforcement officials, both active and retired, public officials, military members, world governments, citizens, friends, and enemies alike are constantly at our gates and calling our phones. Some want a comment and others an exclusive news-bite or interview. One of the more fascinating requests for partnerships are coming from the African continent and its many countries. Some have gone so far as to ditch their invaders religions seeing us as the reincarnation of various Gods. They aren't incorrect however, as their descriptions largely match the priests that came from their regions within the Council of Kerrhe. We aren't reaching out to anyone just yet as we want to let the mood marinate until the 26th where we make our presence known to the world audience. Until then we wait in our cocoon.

The Day is June the 21ˢᵗ, 2011 at 9:00 PM EST

A loud and frantic banging is at my door. I wasn't sleeping but it was jarring after being in a home of such peace for so many days on end. I had been shifting from place to place sometimes as to do works and such with my proxies doing the same via their planes and our overall private network of proxy transportation. I answered the door to find Derek, Shanice, and Ashley at my door telling me that something happened last night; something terrible. I couldn't imagine what could happen and they didn't immediately tell me. I think a part of them was scared at what I would do but I don't know how to react if I don't know what it is they are withholding. They are my family above all else so I'm not going to reach into their memories by grabbing their hands and instead, I will trust them. They told me to come downstairs to my private study. I noticed all of the televisions were off and some of the Riseneya staff were looking at me with such sadness in their eyes; more sadness then when I had taken seven souls to the obliteration of peace that is the chaos realm. I began to get a little tense myself and demanded to know just what happened and that's when Derek said, "It's Goddess and Omar. They were shot last night. Their condition is bad, like really bad but they are still alive Dre'." I yelled, "What the hell were they thinking!" With tears rolling down her face Ashley responded, "I am in pain too – trust me I am. I'm ready to go to the damn hospital right now and bring them back here now but we just found out and we need to do this together. We are your proxies and there are times we do works ourselves even during this radio silence episode. They followed the protocols to fit in and everything but this world is just too damn off-energy for the…"

As my veins grew more luminescent red, I cut her off as well and yelled again, "How the hell did this happen?" Shanice jumped in and said, "Within our communities we feel safe, protected, and appreciated but there is still much work to be done with respect to how some of those in our own culture are still lost and even more so how the authorities interact with us in those moments given their predisposition to violence. Goddess wanted to head out to the new community she was working on and Omar was helping her. You know how Goddess was just getting back in tune with her ancestral talents – she was building this as a surprise to show you what she was creating in honor of that. The Seneca Pink Lake Village is its name and it's near the watershed shores that stretch from Maryland into Virginia. The Nelhenar were there but Goddess, as do us all, don't typically allow them to guard us when in the midst of our own people. They took a single Bentley from the garage and left the community to drive around the surrounding blocks. The village was about to open and when this happens, we always look around the local environment ourselves to gauge the people around it. Apparently, they saw a young teenager digging through a dumpster in an alleyway so they stopped and got out. There were shots fired, the police showed up, more shots were fired, the Nelhenar showed up and a standoff ensued, somehow Goddess and Omar got to the hospital, and that is all we know at this point." When I asked why we weren't contacted, it looks like there were attempts but for some reason it just didn't work out – I think it all just happened so fast that there was little time to think, especially since the world is already on-edge. I asked what hospital and no one knew but the news had reported where they found the ambulance and without hesitation, I told my proxies to not leave the house. I then, shifted to the hospital and began to relentlessly react out of pain. I lifted and choked all of the police at the door – my cauldron of rage taking hold of my actions before I flung them out of my way. I do not have the patience or resolve for them and I need to dissipate my energy in a just way; I won't end them until I have more information on who is responsible and even then, I don't know what I'll do. I demanded to know where Omar and Goddess were being held and the nurses, as if they were waiting for me to arrive showed me to where Omar was. I asked, "Where is Goddess?" but they didn't respond. By the time we got to the end of the hallway where they were, a surgeon met us and said they are both in a coma and we aren't sure that they will make it. One power I do not have is the power over life from death and death from life. But as long as they are alive, and it doesn't matter the state, I can conclave with them. I touched Goddess hands and looked into her recent memories.

They left the car to give the young man money for food as well as a number that him and his family could call for assistance. As they walked up to approach him two men in masks, seemingly out of nowhere held them at gunpoint. To the robbers they looked like rich fools driving through a dangerous city; they had no idea just how important they were. I can't make out the robbers faces and I cannot see any recognizable aspects of their identity. Only one of the robbers has a gun and it's the one pointed at Omar. Omar wrestled the gun away from the robber and during the struggle the gun went off with a loud bang. Goddess looked at herself and realized she wasn't shot, Omar looked at himself and realized he wasn't shot, the robber looked down and realized he wasn't either. However, the other masked robber was shot in the chest and fell to the ground. The robber that initially had the gun ran off while everyone else was in shock but before he fled Omar grabbed him by the facemask and pulled the mask back to expose that he was a young white male. As Omar held the gun, emptying all of the bullets – Goddess went to contain the bleeding of the robber. She removed his facemask and he couldn't have been more than eighteen years old which broke her heart. Omar went to call emergency services to report the incident. Before the EMS ambulance arrived however, the police arrived first – responding to a report of shots fired in a neighborhood known for violence. They pulled up and immediately yelled at Omar to put the gun down. The police perceived the body on the ground to be the innocent one especially since Goddess was hovering that body and Omar still had the gun and mask in his hands. Omar, was still in a bit of shock and went to comply by raising his hands the police, he thought things would deescalate and he would have the ability to tell them what really happened. However, in the heat of the moment, through a lack of empathy, aggressive training, or otherwise they shot Omar four times. He was shot once in the arm, twice in the chest, and once in the leg. As he dropped to the ground with blood spattering all over Goddess, she screamed, "Nooooooo!" There was still a tense feeling in the air and as she stood up without thinking the small black satchel, she had in the dim lighting of the night could have come across as a weapon to overly-aggressive and non-empathetic police forces who didn't value black lives anyway. She was shot twice in the chest and as she falls, she blacks out as she bleeds out. As her eyes begin to close, I feel her pain and anguish. I touched Omar's hand to feel his memories and see it from another angle. To be honest I already knew what happened based on Goddess' view but I had to see it again and I don't know why – I just couldn't believe what I was seeing. Everyone was watching me through the windows now. I could feel their eyes staring at me and their minds wondering how I would react. I turned around and took a deep breath. As I attempted to temper myself Goddess' medical monitor began crashing and as her eyes opened, she looked at me and then as her body convulsed, she died. The medical staff ran in and attempted to revive her as I just stood there with my jaw dropped and my blood boiling. They shocked her, they were screaming for me to step back, they were doing everything in their power to bring her back but after just a few moments, nothing. She laid there, motionless. Her eyes semi-open and lacking spirit or spark. Her arm motionless as it laid on the outside of the bed and the ring I bought for her faced me. The doctor recorded the time of death as June the 22nd, 2011 at 3:06 AM EST.

The Day is June the 22nd, 2011 at 4:05 AM EST

I stand here motionless. I won't let them take her body yet. The metallic smell of the iron in blood and death linger in the air as my pain begins to give way to inconsolable rage and vengeance. The once deafening voices that were a part of me recede into small corners of my mind as the raging fires within me burn all thoughts of restraint. I just stand here motionless. Omar still hasn't awakened yet but they moved him from the room I was in another room. Ashley doesn't know the status of Omar and I can't even bring myself to move an inch from this spot. There's blood dripping from Goddess lifeless body as I continue to just stare with a blank expression on my face – I feel the blankness of emotion yielding into a cauldron of magma at its tipping point; a planet sized rage ready to demolish everything in its path that even slightly resembles the people responsible. I held her hand and shifted back into Riseneya. I took her lifeless body to my innermost sanctum sanctorum and placed her gently on the throne. Ashley asked what happened and I didn't tell her yet as I was just silent. I took her hand and shifted to the hospital so she could at least be with Omar since he was still alive. When we entered the room, we found out that he had died as well. He succumbed to the gunshot wound to the chest that shattered and pierced his heart beyond repair. Ashley completely fell apart. Watching someone that has always been so happy become so befallen with grief was terrifying. I couldn't help but to feel guilty because yet again my friends were getting hurt – nay – dying because of me and the situations I placed them in. We were so close to making something great on this Earth, but I have failed my friends, I have failed everyone. Without saying another word, I took Ashley's hand, guided her over to Omar's lifeless body, and took his hand. I shifted us all to Riseneya and laid his body in the same sanctum antechamber as Goddess'. With a trembling voice, Ashley still in tears, and Derek and Shanice walking into the room where we were, I said, "I have failed you all and I don't know what I just..." I walked off. I told the first staff member I saw to make the arrangements to clean the bodies, and prep them for their journey to the next life. I told them to erect the most significant temple on the grounds that the world has ever seen and after that I walked away; emotionless – I was broken beyond expression. I didn't want to channel Omar or Goddess at the time because the wound was just too fresh in my mind. Instead, I went to deliver the most raging storm to the world. I walked slowly to my interior chambers to put on a garment of pain and mourning; a thick flowing crimson sheath, with the remainder of the outfit being in black and the crown being a ringed crown of gentle but present amber flames pointing downward. With a complete lack of emotion on my face but my head raging with activity, from The First Eye attempting to calm me to my parents attempting the same – but nothing is allowed through right now. Their noise burns to ash among the river of flames coursing through my veins. I haven't felt this level of pain and loss since the passing of my parents; the difference this time is that I will absolutely do something about it. I opened the main Riseneya doors and walked to the main entrance – my crown releasing embers upward while the flames point downward grow in intensity. The camera flashes get more frequent as I walk closer and I stop only for a second to tell the Nelhenar to guard all castles and personnel period – no exceptions, no excuses. I phased through the gate without opening it and pushed everyone back from it using a material wave manipulation; I wasn't gentle. I am broken. I levitate high above all of the remainder of the people in front of the castle and the morning sky begins to give way to thick grey thick clouds. Crimson streaks of lighting pulse through the clouds as the ground beneath everyone shakes. Steam begins to pierce the crust of the earth and cracks begin to form all around the perimeter of the castle grounds where I am standing. A thin line of energy from the core of the Sun pierces my spine igniting my spirit. Everything around the crowd gets hot to the touch as a cocoon of pure impenetrable energy surrounds me in a sphere. More dark greyish purple clouds form and more crimson lighting forms in an ever-growing area around me. The ground is scorching to the touch and much of the crowd begins to panic and scream. The ritual that I am calling is the most powerful one I have ever found and one that I never wanted to use. Its name, Entre Dras Cerena – meaning, 'The Supreme Crimson God-Breaker of Ancestral Pain.' As liquid earth begins to seep from the cracks in the street and the clouds begin to coalesce around the cocoon a loud and deafening growl begins to take hold for miles. I break the cocoon and as it shatters into dust, I hear people screaming as they run for cover – the ash from the cocoon slowly wafting to the ground and blowing in the winds. When the dust clears many of them are looking at me in awe as my skin is now golden with streaks of black, and crimson. My eyes are blood red as a constant stream of blood seeps from them staining whatever they land on. As I drop to the ground onto the magma it splashes but doesn't affect me at all. My crown of fire becomes more pronounced and burns so hot that it becomes a low and intense fire of white flames. Seven thick crimson lightning strikes hit the magma pile next to me and a long staff is created. It has an eternal fire encased with pillars forming a cylinder at its top, it is made of gold and has streaks of crimson pulses throughout it. The bottom of the staff is pure white fire. As I grab the staff and stab it to the ground the magma cools to a smoldering pile of black stone. It cracks and burst after two large shards of crystal break through it and float to my left and my right. On my left floats the Shard of the Vexsen Crimson, a spirit quartz shard with a molten red snake that keeps it together. On my right floats the Shard of the Selkxen Violet, an amethyst shard with a molten white snake that keeps it together. I stand up and the crowd is silent. The beginning of end time is 6:03 AM.

The End Time is June, 22nd, 2011 6:03 AM EST

"I have tried so hard and for so long to practice restraint. I wanted to believe that I didn't have to end up making this decision. For a long time now, I have been battling what I thought were conflicting ideas in my head. Should I take from the nations that have done ill to my people everything? Should I slaughter all who stand in the way of that end? Or should I create a mass of land for my people to live otherwise. I have tried the fusion of them both and for it you murdered my Goddess, my best friend, and an innocent and honorable reporter, Grace Jefferson. You people have acted this way countless times over countless generations and I have felt them all; I feel them all and it sickens me like ten-thousand viruses twelvefold. The more pain you've inflicted on my people the more powerful I become and yet the more unstable my restraint becomes. I have made my decision as to what to do. I will hurt those who have hurt us whether you meant to do it or not; I will punish you with justice. If you are guilty, there is nowhere you can hide from me and I will come for you. I start now and the new era of my justice begins right now. Your stone buildings and institutions will yield to my power in ash, and your sons and daughters for a thousand-thousand generations will tremble at the story of what I will do here. A new era of pain and suffering will begin today and at its conclusion there will be peace for I have deemed it so."

When I grabbed the staff and the Entre Dras Cerena temple at its northern pole shifted from crimson fire into a deep violet and luminous green fire, all of the lights within the eyeline of the horizon of the city were darkened in a loud crackling and spark-filled flash. The only lights that remained were from cell phones, flashlights, crimson and violet lightning strikes, vehicles on the roads, and me. I took a deep and purposeful breath as I began to levitate into the air; the first step of the Vanes Decnes, the vengeful decimation. There is a low-rumble that you can hear for miles as it reverberates within every building within my area. The low-rumbles are colored by sharp cracks that loudly and deeply echo throughout various areas of the dark city – they are complimented by the mechanical sounds of the thunder followed by crimson and violet lightning streaking the sky. The windows in some buildings crackle and burst, shattering their glass shards upon the petrified masses – their light sparkling shimmer as they fall accented by the ever-deepening cracks of concrete giving way to my chaos. Some buildings begin to buckle completely and crash into oblivion, in a thunderous roar, towards the ground. I create the Vanes Decnes Orb of Destruction; a shimmering sphere of violet that pulls chaos from Xenelles Vargelles. As I let it fall to the ground beneath me, it creeps slowly causing dramatic shifts in the environment. Thickened bolts of crimson lightning strike the orb multiple times and the wind from all directions of the city are drawn to it – matched by a faint audible whistle like the sounds of a tornado approaching heard from near the windows of a home. As soon as it touches the ground, all of the buildings fall apart and turn into ash, leaving violet fires in their wake.

The police and military were fearfully shouting commands at this point but it was nothing short of a fly trying to take down an eagle – I can feel that they don't want to be here as they know nothing can stop the truth to which they are bearing witness. The screams of the crowds don't affect me but they are present from every direction. Jets and helicopters are present now, flanking me on all sides they wisped past while more commands were yelled at me – there are at least twenty aerial vehicles confronting me now. I can see their lights from all directions piercing through the darkness of the city.

The Entre Dras Cerena temple's flame turned blue with purple flare ups, granting me the power of vengeful stasis. The aircrafts, stopped where they flew or hovered, became surrounded by a fuchsia stasis field, and they became slowly drawn to me. Pilots were ejecting as I slowly pulled them towards my justice deliverance but I stopped them in the air and pulled them to me, their souls being somewhat ripped from their dense reality and experiencing just a taste of the pain that is Xenelles Vargelles. Some pilots fired missiles and I redirected the explosions into stasis fields and cast them into the atmosphere. The aircraft are so close now that I can see the fear, pain, and panic on the pilots faces. The aircraft get closer still. At this point, they begin to grind into each other – their metal edges screeching and scratching one another. As I formed them into a sphere around me, I took the pilots and crewmen out and let them fall to the ground, slowing them down as they fell to the ground as to not kill them. As the carcasses of the aircrafts surround me, I transmute them into a massive statue of Malcolm X. The massive area around me that I have just reduced to disintegration was now blessed with this silent testimony as the massive inscription says, "By Any Means Necessary."

Just then, two sniper's bullets were shot. They crackled through the air but were subdued by the sounds of thunder rolling through the clouds. As the bullets reached me, they disintegrated into ash but I didn't do this. Still they were a reminder to me that I was on a justified path for the repayment of a debt owed to my people. A gentle collection of voices from within me spoke that my soul was open and that the power of the ancestors now use my soul fire as a vessel of their unified will in tandem with the power of the scroll that is granted by the pain of our collective people – that their intuition is within me and harm shall not penetrate its veil.

The Entre Dras Cerena temple at the northern pole of the staff turned fuchsia, granting me the full powers of vengeful pyranic ash and all of the gunpowder in the area exploded where it was, destroying all of the remaining gunpowder-based military weapons pointed at me in aggression. I yelled a powerful shriek with my voice that was joined by the many ancestors within my soul. A wave of crimson lightning illuminated the sky and as they struck the statue of Malcolm X, black raindrops began to storm. It was at this moment; I began to enact justice everywhere in the world and I swore to continue this justice until justice be done.

The End Time is now June, 22nd 6:30 AM EST

I continued to carry out my decision.

The Day is now September the 3rd, 2034

It took much work to get here and there was much struggle to get here – nay – struggle isn't the right word that can adequately portray what has been the reality. There was significant sacrifice that brought us to where we are today. Some portions of Riseneya and Lexseghn are damaged, and plenty of other areas we owned are equally as torn, both physically and in terms of the sacrifices of the communities. The world looks different today in just these few decades. My friends are much older now, Ashley is 45, while Derek and Shanice are 46. Ashley decided to leave the fold about a decade ago and decided to carry on the work of her best friend Goddess. There's a landmass named 'The Villages of Seneca Pink'; it is home to the cultural ancestral lineage from where Goddess hailed. Ashley made it her own mission to keep that knowledge going for our people. It's under my protection and there it has been thriving. So much so that the remaining proxies decided to follow a similar model with building their respective jurisdictions. Shanice took over the Right Tenant and Derek took over the Left. I established the new Capital country for our new African global collective called, Kerrhe Ele-sei. Ele-sei is an ancient word from the Council of Kerrhe meaning Honored Sacrifice. I thought it was appropriate.

The Capital is a super-massive country that has a land surface area of about three million square miles and functions as the literal heart of our nation. It has so many temples, schools, museums, libraries, art galleries, mystery schools. There so much richness in the ways of economy, arts, justice, law, sciences, self-help, nutrition, healing, mystic rites; I am just so proud. It took so much to get here but it is finally here and it is wonderful; it is inspiring; it is justice.

With respect to what my decision was – just as the Council of Kerrhe left no guidance as to what the correct justice was aside from a few philosophies or its rationale on the general sense of it, I will not record what my decision was here. I will leave that up to you to maul over as you sit with your family, your friends; and amongst your enemies or otherwise. What would you have done? Remove an entire ethnic group or groups from a particular region who took from your people and establish a new land of sanctuary for the healing and prosperity of your people exclusively? Or would you govern the protection of your people from a more political and policy-based standpoint of independent growth by such actions as creating a new landmass for your people to grow, thrive, and live well – while using your powers to defend it against any negative actors or intent? I have made my decision and acted it out, making the ultimate sacrifice in the process.

The First Eye used a ritual similar to this one but it doesn't kill you. It allows you to be a guiding light. In order to call upon The First Eye yourself you must first say his true name, Aulfren, Emaate Mistaynef Memawt, meaning justice reborn anew. Use the ritual tome of The First Guide after you speak his name while in the Lotus Fire Wayfarer position. You must have ancient lotus flower tea from the Northwestern region of the ancient African continent called Dommenes – it is only made by the ancient peoples of the capital city to the far west of its border. They are known as the Rasamenes meaning the ancient Menesi of Dommenes.

One final thing I didn't mention is that the ritual I used to harness such incredible power eventually killed me – once called upon there is no way to remove it as it begins a fire within you that burns until there is nothing left to burn. It does this to anyone who hails it. It is the ultimate sacrifice. My life, my legacy, my struggles; all of it culminated into this moment. Beware to anyone that hails that ritual as it gives you such immense power but it only last for a certain amount of cycles. It draws upon your spiritual energy to function and burns through it like it were fuel, tearing your body and spirit to shreds. I have left all of my work and my life story within this sprawling journal and the scraps of paper stuffed between it. For whomever reads this as the new Mudlahsee, shall use it to guide them and shall see the mistakes I have made as well as the great sacrifice I made to accomplish the successes you now enjoy. When this ritual tears through the little bit of soul matter I have left I will leave this place to a part of spatial states that is locked away, the chaos realm, Xenelles Vargelles. You will not be able to channel me nor will I be able to help you as I am relegated to this realm for the rest of my eternal days. I have fought it for long enough and I will never be too old or too frail but it is time for me to end my story, with freedom.

Sankofa, my successor.

-     Andrel, the First Arbiter of Justice (1987-2034)